THE CURSED SEA

DARK TIDES

BOOK SIX

By
Candace Osmond

CANDACE OSMOND

Cover Work by Majeau Designs
Facebook.com/MajeauDesigns

DEDICATION

To Corey. I know you'd drain the oceans to find me
because I'd do the same for you.

ACKNOWLEDGMENTS

I'm eternally grateful for my readers. Without them, I'd surely be nothing. And to my author bestie, JJ King. My partner in crime who always pushes me to "get it done".

And to my love, Corey. The mastermind behind the design of all my covers, illustrations, maps, merchandise, and the holder of my heart. Thank you for putting up with me.

PROLOGUE

HENRY

Blood. Blood *everywhere*. The flesh of sirens bobbed on the water around me as I stood waist deep in the carnage. It glistened in the setting sun like the bellies of fish; silvery rainbows reflecting everywhere. A stark contrast with the deep, almost black crimson that splattered about. On my jacket, which was heavy and weighed me down as I waded through the battlefield toward the shore. I could feel the beasts' blood pulling at my skin, already drying in the cracks of my face. One hand trembled while the other gripped my sword, the weapon that just laid waste to every siren in the sea. I turned and glanced over my shoulder only to find the wreckage of siren bodies stretching all the way to the horizon.

A dream. I could feel the tethers, the confines and tendrils pulling taut at the edges of my consciousness. A nightmare, really. But one that liberated me every night. But this was the first I'd headed for the shore. When the toe of my boot touched the sand, the grain instantly turned red, and a trail manifested on the beach, leading my line-of-sight straight to the wasteland of bodies from those I loved most in this world. Hands and arms and flesh torn apart, entrails and hair. But...their faces. I dropped to my knees in the sand as a fierce roar erupted from me and I loosened it to the skies above. Their face...everywhere, all turned to gawk at me with permanent looks of terror. Dianna. Gus. Finnigan. Lottie. Little Charlie.

My children.

It was too much to bear. Did I do this? Was this by my hand? I couldn't recall. Couldn't place the beginnings of the nightmare. I'd always entered it after the carnage. To have the horrors thrown in my face, the guilt of what I'd done searing in my veins.

"*It could have been avoided,*" a strange voice scratched in my ear. "*You could have saved them.*"

"How?" I cried. Tears burned through the blood caked to my face.

"*One simple price,*" the voice, now layered with others, replied. "*Your soul.*"

I sprang upright in bed, clutching my chest, desperately gasping for air. Just as I did every night. I wondered if I took a breath at all when I sunk into the repeating nightmare time after time. My lungs burned with every heave and I sat there in the moonlight that covered the half empty bed until they settled. It wasn't until then that I realized the bed wasn't as empty as I'd thought. They huddled together, two little lumps under the sheet, and I pulled it back with hesitation. But when I saw their sleeping faces, so perfect, so innocent, I nearly cried at the relief.

It was just a dream.

I ran a hand through my damp hair as a shiver blew over my clammy skin. A quick glance at the clock told me it was three in the morning. Another day was upon us, which marked three since we came through the portal without Dianna. I winced at the thought of her name. Just the mere sound of it was enough to undo me. Constance had said to be patient, to wait for the Keepers to do their work. They'd find a way to send her back. It was their job.

But, with each passing hour, I grew more and more weary of the witch's ability to police time. She should be back by now. She should be home.

But part of me worried she was lost forever.

CHAPTER ONE

DIANNA

It'd been three days since I lost Henry and the kids to the other side of the portal. Three days that I've wandered the grounds of Finn's childhood home in a never-ending daze. The Artair Keep. It was beautiful there. Grassy knolls and endless skies surrounding a massive stone structure that seemed to stretch on forever. Decades of Artairs and their contributions to the home all summed up in a series of small castle-like buildings that circled the main house where we stayed. All of it contained within a high wall of stone and iron that protected what was precious to them.

Freya's coop of females littered the keep, tending to daily duties like cooking and cleaning, and chopping wood. Neither of them bothered to pay attention to me, or perhaps I didn't give them the chance. The stranger, the zombie who walked the grounds with no purpose. I wondered what they thought of me. Then again, the women of the Artair Keep lived in a world all their own with duties and such. They relied on no man to keep the place running, and I admired them for it. This was a haven, and I was lucky to see it during its prime.

Still...my heart ached for my family.

At least I knew they were safe and sound at home. Mom was there. And the kids had Henry. I just worried for him, for the man I loved. He had no one. I was his world as he was mine, and now he was stuck three hundred years in the future without me. In a future that was still so new to him. With no way of knowing whether I was safe. I tried not to think of the lengths he'd go to in order to get back to me and could only hope that he wouldn't try. The kids needed him.

I knew what it was like to lose a mother to the sea and the tragedy had tainted me from an early age, morphed my mind, my will, every fibre of who I came to be. The difference was that my father descended into the darkness of mourning. I was alone even when I wasn't. Arthur and Audrey had Henry. A strong man, both inside and out. I prayed every minute that he was present for them and their little hearts.

But I knew better. Knew my pirate king would tackle both. He'd tend to the kids' every whim while also tearing the earth apart in search of a way back to me. Because that's exactly what I had done. So many years ago. When the magic of time sent me back to the future, injured and heartbroken with life growing inside of me. I did everything to get back to him and nearly killed us all in the process. I couldn't let Henry do that. So, I had to get back to him before he did something stupid.

I just hoped the witches had good news for me.

I leaned against a short fence made of strong and shaven logs as I watched Lottie hang laundry out on a line in the distance. It killed me to witness her grieving so silently. Losing her unborn baby had changed her, but losing the man she loved had turned her so inward that she almost seemed robotic at times. As stubborn as she was beautiful, she had no idea how to properly process her emotions and, try as I might, she wouldn't let me in. Instead, she threw herself into work. Keeping her hands busy so her mind didn't have to be.

Or perhaps she was refusing to let in the dread that loomed over us all about tonight. Gus' funeral. It'd been a rather rough three days. I'd spent some time with the witches at first, trying to find a way back, to find a loophole. While Lottie locked herself in her room and grieved. She wasn't ready to put him to rest, so we prepared his body and secured it away in one of the outbuildings until she was ready. But three days was long enough to leave a corpse. It was time to face it, whether she wanted to.

So, tonight we'd bury a friend, and tomorrow I'd meet with the witches again, to find a loophole that would allow my soulless self to travel to the future. I just prayed they found something. Otherwise, my only other option was to take Benjamin up on his offer to bring me down South to meet with someone named David Jones, a soul dealer. My rational mind fought it, but part of me knew who he really was. The mythical being, the legend of the sea. Davy Jones. Who else could it possibly be?

"Are ye always this much of a deep thinker?" Freya asked as she appeared by my side and leaned over the fence. Her fiery locks blew softly about her freckled face. "Ye seem lost, Dianna."

I guffawed and turned over, resting my back against the fence so I could gaze out over the moors beyond the keep. "Aren't I?"

Freya sighed. "I suppose ye are, in a way."

"In many ways," I corrected. She was silent as I gnawed at the inside of my cheek. "Serves me right for messing with time, I guess. The sirens had warned me, more than once."

"The Keepers will help ye," she assured me.

I shook my head and closed my eyes. "God, I hope so."

"If nae," she said with certainty, "I can have a ship readied in two days. To take ye wherever ye need to go."

I tipped my head to look her square in the face. "I

know. And I appreciate it, but I'm not sure Henry could stand to wait while I sail to the Caribbean on a fool's errand."

"Fool's errand?"

I cringed inwardly. While Ben had offered me a solution, I just didn't believe in it. He'd known this David Jones over a hundred years ago. Myth or not, how could I be sure we'd find him now? What if we sailed all the way down South only to meet a dead end? I couldn't afford to waste that much time. And I didn't want to put myself in a desperate position of begging the sirens for help. I swore I'd never deal with them again.

So, I just shrugged it off. "No matter. All I can do right now is focus on one moment at a time." I tipped my chin toward Lottie in the distance.

Freya hummed in agreement. "Aye, the funeral. Poor Charlotte, me heart breaks for her. So much loss for one person to endure."

I thought of my own loss then. A much different beast than my friends', but a painful weight, nonetheless. Losing my mother, my father, Aunt Mary, Gus, even old man Pleeman who'd given his life to save mine aboard The Black Soul. Lives and souls and hearts all breaking in my hands, at my touch. It was all too much to bear at times. I didn't want that for my friend. I wished I could take that burden for her.

I pushed off the fence and sucked in a deep, exhausted breath. "She's stronger than you think. She just needs...*time*." Was I talking about Lottie or myself? I decided it didn't matter and headed back toward the main house to wait for the sun to go down.

***

The fire was hypnotic. Hot and blaring with the rage it held within the billowing flames. The heap of burning wood held up a bed of perfect square of stacked logs that cradled Gus' body as it became engulfed in dances of orange and yellow. After Finn had said a few words, the five of us stood evenly spaced around the pyre, encased in our own silences under the midnight sky. It was a clear night, the stars shone down on us like twinkling eyes. Watching our pain, witnessing Lottie's agony she kept welled up inside. She stood alone in her corner, uninviting, unwanting of our condolences. She just stared unblinking at the flames, and they lit up her face with a fiery rage.

"That's a sight I hope to never see again," Benjamin whispered as he sidled up next to me.

I crossed my arms tightly across my chest. "What? The sight of our friend's body reducing to ash or the sight of our other friend keeping herself together by threads?"

He heaved a long sigh. "Neither, I guess."

"God, just look at her," I whispered and motioned toward Lottie. She was a shell. Disjointed, cut-off, blankly staring at her beloved going up in flames, her arms wrapped tightly across her chest as if she refused to let the pain reach her heart. I knew exactly how she felt. It was the only way I was keeping myself together after losing Henry and the kids through the portal. "I'm worried she's going to spiral after I leave, and I won't be here to help her."

"So, you think the witches will have a solution for you tomorrow?" I tried to ignore the hint of reluctance in his tone. He didn't want me to go, I knew that. But neither of us would dare admit it.

I just tilted my head to the side and gave him a warm look layered with a useless apology. "I-I have to get back to my kids, Ben."

He let his gaze fall to the ground as he nodded slowly. "I know." The words were barely a whisper in the night breeze.

I loosened my arms from the tight cross they held over my chest and gripped his arm, causing his muscles to tense under his shirt at my touch. Benjamin stared down at me from his towering height, his long brown hair blanketing the sides of his solemn face. "If I could stay, I would. But my entire life is on the other side of that portal."

He just nodded and his jaw gave a slight tremble as he turned his attention on Lottie. He nudged his head toward where she stood alone. "You best go over. She won't ask, you know that, but she needs you."

I gave his arm a reassuring squeeze, and he placed a firm, calloused hand over mine. The reflection of the flames burned in those deep brown eyes as they peered down at me with a sort of longing that was hard to ignore. But I had to. Benjamin was my friend, and someone had to maintain the line that he made no secret of his yearning to cross.

I walked across the cool, damp grass and stood next to Lottie. She didn't give so much as a blink to acknowledge my presence, but she didn't send me away, either. So, I remained and rubbed warmth into my arms where the fire didn't touch. I fixated on her eyes, gazing unblinkingly at the body on the pyre. Her husband. She seemed like a porcelain doll, so still and perfectly beautiful. Every inch of her face flawless under a mess of blonde waves that hung like a curtain around it. But underneath it all was a woman writhing in agony. I could feel her pain like a wave that pulsed outward from her body.

"What was it all for?" she croaked quietly, her lips the only thing that moved.

"What do you mean?" I asked.

She gave a tight shrug. "What the hell was the point of any of it?" Wetness pooled in her blue eyes. "Of him loving me, or me loving him?" She wiped at the single tear that broke free and streamed down her cheek. "It's always life or death. Or loss." Lottie sniffled then and finally set her pained gaze on me. "You lose Henry and the kids—"

"They're not lost," I quickly amended. Surprised at the little dose of panic that punched me in the gut. "I-I didn't lose them, they're safe at home."

I'm the one who's lost, I thought to myself.

Lottie turned her attention back to the fire. "Gus is gone. And...I loved him more than anything in this world."

I didn't have the right words for my friend. Nothing I could say would ease her pain or help with the grief. She had to move through the motions on her own, find herself again. However long that took. So, I continued to just stand with her, to let her know I was there. She wasn't alone.

But Lottie gave a long sigh as she tightened her jacket around her torso and turned her back to the fire. She placed a hand on my shoulder and struggled to look me in the eye. "It's only a matter of time before you leave me, too."

I opened my mouth to speak, but nothing came out as I watched my friend disappear toward the main house. The pyre behind me raged on, heating my back and soaking into the skin beneath my clothes. The burning logs shifted and what remained of Gus' body sunk deeper into the flames. And in that moment, I realized...I couldn't leave. Not yet. Not when my family was perfectly safe at home and my friend—my other family—was here, suffering so greatly. Lottie needed me. I could afford to wait a few more days.

I just prayed Henry didn't do something stupid in the meantime.

CHAPTER TWO

HENRY

"Daddy?" a tiny, musical voice called from somewhere. "*Daddy!*" it rang again, this time cutting through the fog that surrounded my mind. That *always* surrounded my mind these last few days.

I blinked away the scape of deep, dark worry that constantly plagued me and glanced around the kitchen where I stood. Alarmingly, I couldn't recall the motions that had brought me to this room. Audrey tugged at my leg and peered up at me with those giant sparkling deep brown eyes. Dark, just like mine. I thanked the heavens these last few days that she never inherited her mother's mesmerizing doe-eyed stare. I wasn't sure I'd be able to handle looking at it every day.

I plastered on a smile. For her. For the kids. Because I had to be strong for them. Because...Dianna would want me to. "Yes, my princess?"

She brightened. "Can I have my apple slices now?"

I followed her line of sight to my hands atop of the kitchen island where I held a half-sliced apple. A knife in the other. I couldn't even remember fetching the items. Couldn't recall the steps I'd taken to washing and slicing the apple into the little pink plastic dish that awaited. I shook off the remnants of a daydream and set the knife in the sink before handing the tiny bowl to my daughter.

"Here you go," I said and stole a slice.

"Daddy!" she exclaimed with a giggle.

I chuckled and lobbed off a bite. The juices alerting my taste buds that it'd been the first thing to touch my tongue that day. "Does your brother want some?"

"I dunno." She shrugged and skipped off, so blissfully unaware that her mother wasn't just away, she was lost in time. Neither of them seemed to remember their little trip to the past or their time with the siren. The portal, thankfully, didn't seem to register with their flimsy grip on reality, either.

"Can you ask him?" I called after her as she disappeared around the corner.

I waited for the inevitable and exaggerated sigh. Then her answering *yes*. I opened the fridge to fetch another apple and held it under the water that rushed from the faucet. I chuckled quietly to myself as I recalled those first months here in the future. When Dianna brought me…home. Things like lighting, plumbing, hot showers each day, automobiles. I met them all with a curious mind, but it was her that made my transition to the future as good as it was. Dianna, my whole world. My other half. The woman who came to the past and saved me from the shackles of my former life.

And now she was stuck in the same wretched past she'd plucked me from. With no way home to us. My only solace was knowing that she was with friends. She was safe. But it wouldn't stop me from finding a way to get her back.

Eventually.

I'd tried using the sun and the moon on the water trick the very day we returned. Just hours after I'd stepped through that portal with Arthur and Audrey. But either the sea didn't see fit to send me back, or it simply didn't work for everyone. Because I'd desperately bobbed on the water's surface for hours. Waiting for the ocean to open up and swallow me whole. When I'd finally hauled the rowboat up on the beach behind our house, Constance was there to greet me with a look of concern.

"*It should have worked,*" she'd said, bewildered.

That was five days ago.

I filled the slogging hours by tending to the kids. Constance suggested keeping them home from preschool for a while until they could properly adjust to the events they surely couldn't comprehend. But after these last few days, it was clear that Arthur and Audrey escaped unscathed. Their usual childlike cheer and wonder filled the house, and I breathed a sigh of relief nearly every minute. But tomorrow they were heading back to preschool, and I'd be left alone with my thoughts, my worries. The urge to flee to the past and save the woman I loved.

Just wait, Constance told me, *the Keepers will find her a way back. It's their solemn duty.*

But I couldn't wait. Every second was one too long without Dianna. And what if the witches had already told her there was no hope? No way back home. What then? Was I expected to just live out my days, always wondering, never knowing what happened to her? My fist clenched at my side as I retreated to that far corner of my mind where my worry for Dianna lived. Where I hid it from the children.

"Dad?" another voice spoke, once again pulling me from that spiral.

I blinked and smiled down at Arthur, immediately realizing that I'd gripped the edge of the small blade I held, and warm drops of red trickled down my wrist. With haste, I stuck my bleeding hand under cold water, while keeping that unbothered look for my son.

"Sorry, little man," I said and grabbed some paper towel to wrap the wound that burned across my palm. With my other hand, I passed Arthur his bowl of apple slices.

He peered up at me questionably, while clutching the little bowl to his chest. Those big, dark eyes like that of a sweet doll. So perfect and innocent.

"You okay, Dad?" His stubby fingers reached out to grab my leg. "You gots an owie?"

I rustled the blonde curls atop his head and crouched down to his eye level. "Dad is fine, I just got a little cut. You go finish watching the movie with your sister before I get you ready for a bath, okay?"

His soft chin bounced up and down and I hugged him close. Breathed him in. My son. My boy. He and his sister were everything to me; the two greatest gifts Dianna had ever given me aside from her heart. As I watched him skip off around the corner to join his sister, my eyes stung with tears. Tears I would not shed because I knew their mother wouldn't want them. She was fine. We were fine.

We just weren't together.

After I got the twins to bed, tucked in, and sleeping soundly, I grabbed a sweater and headed down to the beach to clear my head. The sound of the waves and the smell of the cool night air always soothed my soul. If I closed my eyes long enough and pushed away the sounds of the modern world around me, I could almost remember what it felt like to stand on the deck of The Devil's Heart.

I stuffed my hands in the pockets of my thick knitted sweater and the wound on my palm burned. I removed the makeshift bandage, thinking how Dianna would have done a much better job, and stuck my entire hand in the seawater. I winced at the sting, but it subsided soon enough, and I swirled my hand back and forth, letting the cool saltwater cleanse the gash.

The full moon lit up the surface of the ocean like liquid silver drops, and I focused on the dark, ethereal beauty of it rather than the utter agony I harboured inside. If this was even a fraction of what Dianna must have felt, so many years ago, when she'd been ripped from me and sucked back to the future...then she was much stronger than I. The uncertainty she was left with, not knowing my fate or anyone else of our crew. At least I had that— the knowing, the assurance that she was safe and sound with our friends.

Still...I'd once promised I'd drain the oceans to find her.

I couldn't just sit and wait. What if the day never came that she returned to me? What if she was waiting on the other side, praying that I was coming to save her, and I never showed up? She'd come for me if the roles were reversed. A new fire burned in my gut, rising and spreading up through my chest. I had to at least try. I couldn't wait, couldn't be patient as Constance asked. I knew what I had to do. I just needed to get to the past first.

So, I headed back to the house and got to work.

***

The warm afternoon sun blared in through the large window in the dining room, melting the damp chill that hovered in the old house. I stood with a tea in hand, letting the steam waft up across my face as I stared out at the sparkling water in the distance. The twins were at preschool, leaving our beachside home in painful silence. But it gave me time to think, time to plot all the ways I could save Dianna.

The front door swung open and Constance walked in, carrying a tray of freshly baked goods and a bulky tote bag.

"Afternoon," she greeted and set the tray down on the kitchen island. She looked at me expectantly. "Aren't you leaving?"

I took a sip of my tea and placed it with a clink on the stone countertop. "Leaving?"

Constance checked her watch. "Didn't you need me to watch the kids after school today?"

A rush of adrenaline sprang to life in my chest. "Yes!" I cursed under my breath and tossed the rest of my tea down the sink as I checked the clock. "I completely lost track of time."

After weeks and weeks of rifling through the things in Dianna's office, through the things that she shared with her mother, I'd found nothing that looked like a way to travel through time. Nothing except the contact for a man in Corner Brook who collected rare and obscure things from the sea. Trinkets from shipwrecks, old maps, photos, and–according to his website–some of the rarest pearls in the world.

I was hoping they'd be the elusive siren pearls, the ones that granted wishes. But I couldn't say anything to Constance until I knew for sure. She'd warned me to stay put and let the witches help Dianna, warned me of the risks that came with messing with time.

"Best to get on the road now while you have a few good hours of sunlight left," she said, already unloading the bakery treats she brought for the kids. "What time will you be back?"

I shrugged into my black leather jacket and plucked my bike helmet from the closet by the door. "Hopefully sometime late this evening."

"Remind me what you're doing, again?" she asked with a curious tone.

I smiled. A poor attempt to assure her I wasn't up to anything. "Just doing some shopping." I leaned over and pecked her cheek before turning toward the door. "Kiss the kids goodnight for me."

"Be safe," she called as I shut the door behind me.

I hauled my bike out from where it parked alongside the house and secured my helmet. After many failed attempts at teaching me to drive a car, Dianna thought a motorcycle would be a better fit.

And she'd been right. Easier to drive, easier to manoeuvre, but I also found solace in the freedom it gave me. The wind in my face, my hair, airing out my thoughts as I flew down the highway to my destination.

After an hour and a half, I took a turn and exited toward Corner Brook. A neighbouring town that bustled with charm. It sat atop a hill and overlooked a large harbour. I recognized the landmarks—the mountains, the shoreline—I'd been there dozens of times. In the time of my past. Now, here in the future, Dianna and I often came to Corner Brook to do some shopping. Once, she'd taken me to Marble Mountain, the ski resort that sat next to the town, and she'd taken so much pleasure in witnessing my attempt to learn how to ski.

I shook away the pleasant memories as I dismounted my bike and set the helmet on the seat. I couldn't afford to dwell on things like that, not when those memories so easily reduced me to the dark and emotional mess I refused to be.

Not when Dianna needed me.

I entered the little hole-in-the-wall antique shoppe that sat snugged in the middle of a row of various specialty stores downtown, and an old brass bell signalled my arrival. A middle-aged man appeared from behind a curtain that hung on the other side of a counter.

"Good day," he greeted kindly and pushed up the glasses that edged down the tip of his nose. "Can I help you?"

"Yes," I replied and sauntered around the store, crowded with trinkets and collectibles of all sorts. Old anchors, ship's wheels, and other things from the turn of the century. It gave a homey feel, something familiar. Something I could relate to in this still-strange and modern world. "We spoke on the phone." I reached out a hand to shake. "Henry White."

The man brightened. "Oh, yes! The gentleman looking for rare pearls." He dipped down below the glass countertop that divided us and fetched a small wooden box. He set it down in front of me and opened it. "Here we go. Some of the oldest and rarest ocean pearls in the world."

I peered inside the box, fingered through the dozens. Black, cream, pink, grey. Every colour one would expect. But it wasn't the colours I was looking for. It was that...*feeling*. That otherworldly sheen, the odd weight of them. Like cool tin. Slick with magic.

But these were just...pearls. Real ones.

I sighed disappointedly as I rolled a large grey one between my fingers.

"Not what you're looking for?" the man asked.

I shook my head and returned the pearl to the box. "No," I replied. Defeat heavy on my chest. "I'm afraid not." I gave him a single nod. "I thank you for your time."

"Well, if there's ever anything I can do, anything I can find for you, you know where to contact me," he assured cheerily.

I shook his hand and left the store, pausing a moment to take in a deep breath of fresh air. I was a fool to think this simple merchant would possess enchanted siren pearls, but the weight of pure disappointment still soured in my gut. This was my only lead.

I couldn't go home yet. Not when my body was tense with the anger that pulsed through my veins. So, as my bike roared to life, I slipped on my helmet and took off. I drove up and down every winding road in Corner Brook. Parked down by the harbour and walked the entire length of the beach, cursing and yelling at the sea, before turning back again. The sun had long gone down. The kids would be in bed, and Constance was probably worrying.

So, I headed home. Empty-handed.

I took my time on the highway. Driving in the dark of night came with its risks, especially in Newfoundland. Moose often ran across the highway, appearing out of nowhere like silent beasts unknowingly causing car wrecks and taking lives.

When I finally pulled up to our home, something caught my eye in the headlight. A figure standing on the porch. I shut off the engine and ran over.

"Christ, Audrey," I said, trying to remain calm, but panic seared my limbs. "What are you doing out here, princess?"

She just stood there, staring blankly at the space over my shoulder. Her floor-length nightgown dripped with water, soaked up to her knees, and her bare feet stood in a puddle of water. She must have been sleepwalking again. An unpleasant habit she'd gained upon our return from the past. I made a note to install some locks higher on the doors.

I shrugged out of my jacket and wrapped it around her entire body before scooping her up into my arms. She never woke, but immediately softened in my grasp as she molded to my warm chest. She was like ice in my hands.

I entered the house as quietly as I could. Constance was asleep on the sofa next to the woodstove, totally unaware. I didn't blame her, though. This wasn't the first time Audrey wandered in her sleep, and I knew she did it with an unnerving silence. I carried my daughter upstairs and set her on the bed while I grabbed some dry pyjamas from the dresser and an extra blanket from the closet she and her brother shared. Only when I removed her wet and sandy nightgown, and clothed her in fresh garments, did she wake.

"Daddy?" she murmured tiredly and rubbed at her eyes.

I sat next to her, the tiny mattress sagging under my weight. "You were walking in your sleep again," I told her in a gentle breath. I wiped the damp hair from her confused face. "What were you doing outside?"

She blinked at me, then stared out the window. "The ocean was whispering to me." She laid back on her pillow with a carefree yawn. "I had to go see what it wanted."

My neck turned, and I shot my hard gaze out the window, almost glaring at the sea in our backyard. Panic pumped hot in my blood. When I looked back at my daughter, she'd already sunk back into a deep sleep. Her cherub-like face slack and soft. Content. I breathed a sigh of relief and leaned over to lay a kiss on her forehead. But when I pulled away, something around her neck caught the light of the moon that shone in from the window.

Two pearls. Secured around Audrey's little neck with a thin braid of seaweed.

My heart sprang to life in my chest, refusing to settle down. Was that...what I thought it was? What I'd been searching for all this time? I removed the string from her neck, careful not to wake her, and rolled the pearls between my fingers.

The odd weight, the slick and otherworldly feeling of magic that coated them. This was it. Two pearls. One to leave, one to come back. I clutched them tightly in my hand. Finally, I could save Dianna, I could bring her home.

I'd wait until morning so I could make arrangements with Constance to care for the twins in my absence and to explain what I'd found. Because I was going back in time to save Dianna, and I wasn't coming back without her.

CHAPTER THREE

DIANNA

I gripped the thick leather reins as my horse came to a halt at the treeline where the Keepers asked to meet. Late last night, while pacing the floors of my quarters at the Artair Keep, a piece of parchment floated in through the window and landed gracefully on the bed. When I unrolled it, I found only a simple instruction. Where to meet and what time.

And so there I was.

I laid awake all night, wondering what news the Keepers would have for me. What method of time travel did they find for someone like me? Someone without a soul. Or would they bear bad news? I considered that option, but then reasoned with myself. Surely, they wouldn't make me ride across the moors just to deliver bad news. I liked to think they had the decency to come to me, in that case.

So, I held on to that flimsy hope of good news. Kept the sweet faces of my children at the forefront of my mind. Let the memory of Henry's touch linger on my skin. It was the only way to stay grounded. To not the let agony of our separation weigh me down.

I waited a few more minutes as my horse calmly trotted up and down part of the treeline. Our breaths forming as mist and molding together before drifting upward to the sky. My skin bristled with the chill of the early evening, and goosebumps scoured up my back just as I caught the faintest glimpse of movement in the trees. A dark figure— no, *three*—slowly emerged and stepped into the moonlight that covered the lands.

"Dianna Cobham," Ingrid spoke firmly. I couldn't read her. "We have some questions."

Something about her tone didn't sit right in my gut. I focused on the faint lines of some intricate tattoo that covered her chest, poking up from the white long-sleeved tunic she wore. Simple things. Like one of the witches; her bald head and eyes blackened in circles of some kind of paint or dye. The three of them rode beautiful black stallions with intricate braids in their manes and tails. Raw beauty. The entire sight of them.

"What do you want to know?" I asked, calm-like.

Ingrid glanced between her two sisters. Then to me, with that stony look. "When ye traded yer soul, what were the exact terms?"

I swallowed nervously. "With the siren?" Ingrid nodded, and I writhed my hands together. "I traded it to save my husband from the siren's grasp. Why? You'd already asked me this."

She took a deep breath and crossed her arms. "And there were nae other terms? Just a...direct exchange?"

I shook my head. "What do you mean? What other terms?"

"Often, a siren or Fae will make a deal, but add a condition. A loophole that would allow ye to reverse the deal if ye so wished."

I thought about it, about that fateful day in the siren's den. "No," I breathed. "I'm afraid not." Ingrid leaned back and sighed. "What? What does that mean?"

She glanced at the other sister, one with a mess of long brown hair and a beautiful face. She just nodded at Ingrid.

"What's going on?" I asked.

"Dianna," Ingrid started. "We considered every possibility. But, ultimately, the only correct solution is for ye to get yer soul back from the Fae."

"How am I supposed to do that?"

She crossed her arms over her horse's neck and leaned forward. "That's up to ye. But I reckon it widnae come without a price. Another trade of some sort."

"No," I said with the smallest hint of a tremble. "I'm done making deals with sirens and mermaids and pirates. The whole lot of it!" I took a long deep breath in and out. "I just...want to go home with my husband and kids."

Ingrid slowly shook her head. "Then, I'm sorry, Dianna. But we do nae deal in souls. Only the sanctity of time." She waited a beat and, when I didn't respond, she added, "But if ye can manage to get ye soul back, then we'll gladly send ye home."

I gradually nodded. "Okay." My lips pursed as I let it sink in. "I'll just...find a way. One that doesn't involve the Fae."

Ingrid inclined her head toward me. "Then we wish ye luck, Dianna Cobham." She gave her horse's reins a little flick, and the beast stood at attention. "Ye'll surely need it."

I stayed in place long after the three of them disappeared into the forest. I couldn't ride all the way back. Not yet. Not when my world was crashing and spinning around me. I tied the horse to a tree, and I sat down at the base of the trunk. My back molded to the rounded, jagged bark as I let the weight of defeat crush of disappointment consume me.

I had to sail for months on the ocean once again. The same ocean that nearly took my life, more than a time or two. All on the slight chance that Ben may be right about this David Jones guy. And, as much as I tried not to think it, some rational part of my mind knew who it was, or who it might very well be. I mean, David Jones? An immortal dealer of souls who also happens to have a set of keys to the underworld? Even after all these years, after everything I'd seen and experienced, my mind still insisted on fighting against the realization. The truth that blared in my face.

My only hope of returning to the future was to sail across the sea in search of...*Davy Jones*.

I made no sound, none at all. Just laid there, dying on the inside. But there was something new inside of me. A strange, tangible void that lived in the back of where my soul used to be. A sort of darkness, a black switch-like thing that I desperately wanted to touch. I reached out for it and pressed my mind's hand against the black square and immediately...everything was quiet. As if the world had been shut off with a light switch. *Snap!* Silence.

The world around me darkened, and I spun downward into an empty but welcoming void. And that's where I happily remained. Basking in the comfort of nothingness. I could stay there forever.

I had no idea how much time had passed when the firm grip of hands on my body was shaking me awake. My eyes slowly pried open to find that the sun had come up and my horse was nowhere to be found. I was still at the base of the tree I'd laid down at, but my body was stiff with the soreness of laying on the ground all night. Something shook me again, and I finished swimming to the surface of my consciousness where my gaze landed on Benjamin.

"Christ!" He blew out a tense breath of air and sat back on the ground as he wrung a hand through his tousled hair. "Dianna, what are you *doing* here?"

I blinked away the last of the sleep from my eyes and tried to find the words. Buried somewhere deep inside. I'd laid down because my emotions had been crushing me. But now...they were gone. A soothing silence left in their wake.

"I-I...fell asleep."

His thick brown eyebrows raised high as his eyes widened in disbelief. "You *fell asleep*?" I just shrugged. "When your horse returned to the Keep without you, we didn't know what to think! What happened? What did the Keepers say?"

I shook my head, slowly, heavily. As if the very movement took a great effort. I stared down at my hands in my lap. The witches hadn't given me good news, and I knew I should feel *something*; sadness, anger, loss. But I felt...nothing. Nothing except the reeling sensation of a strange and dark freedom. My rational mind urged me to go back, turn the switch on, but I couldn't do it. Not now.

Benjamin rubbed his large hand over his face and watched me. He practically brimmed with questions but didn't dare pry further. I thought about what I must look like to him. Lost, perhaps traumatized. Little did he know the comfortable emptiness I swam in on the inside.

He hopped to his feet, his heavy brown leather boots clunking against the hard round. He bent down and held a hand out to me. "Come on," he said and motioned for me to take his hand. "Let's get you back."

I slipped my palm across his and he gripped my hand firmly as he led me over to the horse he'd rode on. Without a word, he hoisted me up on the horse's back and followed behind me, squishing me up against the horn. I let out a huff as it drove into my stomach and his thick arm wrapped around me from behind, dragging me back to sit tightly against his chest.

Benjamin kicked his heels and flicked the reins before the stallion took off across the Scottish countryside. A blanket of orange and purple followed us the entire way back until it morphed to a lovely blue that lit up the lands. The warmth of Ben's body soaked into me until it filled the gaping hole in my chest. Chased away the icy darkness that had taken residence in me under that tree. I relished in it, the warmth, the hot steam that seemed to seep from him. His pounding heartbeat blaring against my back. His breath on my neck, sending a tickle of shivers over my skin.

I was hyper-aware of Ben's muscled arm around my torso, holding me securely in place. But when we arrived at the Keep and he slid off the horse, taking all that lovely warmth with him, the stark cold that snapped tight inside of me washed all the treacherous thoughts from my mind. What was I doing? This was *Benjamin*. He was like a brother to me. Nothing more. But the eerie darkness where my soul used to be now screamed for his warmth.

I had to get back to Henry. Fast.

I couldn't very well stay here in the past while my family, my very reason for living, were on the other side. In the future. Mourning the loss of their mother and wife. The kids would be too young to really grasp it, but Henry would spiral right about now. With days gone by and no sign of my return.

I stopped and stood in place, in the wide-open meadow by the stables, and retreated farther into my mind, searching for...what was I searching for? Oh, right...guilt. Sorrow. Sadness. But, as I raked over every inch of me, I found...

...nothing.

No emotions at all. My rational mind *knew* how Henry and the kids must be feeling. I *knew* what Henry was probably doing to get back to me. Rifling through every piece of paper in my office. Just as much as I knew how I should be feeling myself. But there was nothing. Just a tangible emptiness.

Be thankful, a voice whispered.

Startled, I whipped around, immediately nauseated by the rush of feeling...*something*. But there was no one to be found. My ears picked up the faint noise of Benjamin in the stables, putting the horse away and tending to other things.

A chill crept down my spine and I headed into the stables, glancing over my shoulder every few seconds for a sign of who—or what—may have whispered in my ear. Could I have imagined it? No, because I could almost still feel the brush of a breath that touched my face.

I leaned against a post and chewed at my lip as I contemplated my next move. Benjamin moved with ease, his tall and wide frame bending and lifting as he cleaned things up. He grabbed a large bundle of hay and began tearing it apart for the horses as he looked at me. His muscles moving beautifully under the thin white tunic shirt he wore.

"What's the matter?" he asked me. "Thought you'd be running off to the sirens by now."

"What?" I asked, confused.

"The witches," he said. "They couldn't help you, right?" I nodded and let my gaze fall to the ground. "Then, unless you want to take me up on my offer of sailing South, the sirens are your only hope of returning to the future." When I didn't respond, he added doubtfully, "Or...am I wrong?"

He sauntered over to me and when the toes of his heavy leather boots neared mine, I looked up. Benjamin peered down at me from his ridiculous height, a mix of so many things found in his inviting eyes. Yearning, friendship, torment. I wanted nothing more than to satisfy that gaze.

No! I chastised myself and wrapped my arms tightly around my torso as I took a step back. "I can't make any more deals with the beasts of the sea. Look what good it's done me."

He shrugged and straightened a saddle that was

slung over a hook. "Yeah, but we're talking about your soul here, Dianna." Why couldn't I speak? I searched for words but had no reply. "Don't you want to go home?"

No, stay here, that same voice cackled in a whisper. I stifled the rush of goosebumps that scratched under my skin, making my blood boil. Ben gave me a curious look, but I took a deep breath and held it together.

I cleared my throat, but words still stumbled out hoarsely. "Ben, I need your help."

He straightened. "With what?"

My hands wrought together in front of me. "Can you truly lead me to this David Jones person?"

His thick brows pinched together, and he examined me. "Yes," he said slowly and put his hands on his hips. "I can bring you where you need to be."

"But what are the chances of us actually finding him?" I pried further. "I can't–" My chest expanded with a deep, calming breath. "I need it to be a sure thing before I devote the time to sail across the ocean."

Benjamin gave me a pitiful look. "Is anything in this life a *sure thing*?"

I guffawed. "I suppose not."

"I can take you across the Atlantic, Dianna," he assured and then neared me, so close his breath touched my face. "And I can bring you to the exact spot where you'd find David Jones. But, whether he wants to help isn't up to me or you. So, the real question you should ask is...is that a risk you're willing to make?"

I dared meet his fixed stare and swallowed nervously, but masked the unwelcome feeling with a weak grin. "What would Freya think of you sailing across the ocean with me?"

Benjamin chuckled. "Freya is very...hospitable." When I arched a brow, he rolled his eyes. "I mean, she's lovely. And welcoming. And has helped all of us immensely. But she's not...she's...a good friend."

I inhaled deeply, accepting the next choice I had to make. "In that case, I would be forever grateful if you'd help me sail down South and get my soul back."

He took my hand and gave a mocking bow. An unexpected giggle bubbled in my chest, quickly replaced by a searing sensation that spread to the tips of every limb as he brought the back of my hand to his lips.

"Whatever the lady needs," he said jokingly.

But it didn't feel like a joke to me. No, the otherworldly presence that roamed around my insides relished at his touch, at the attention, and the feel of Ben's soft lips on the skin of my hand. When he released it, my arm fell to my side, and I breathed a sigh of relief while my insides screamed for more.

This was going to be a long trip.

CHAPTER FOUR

Even though I had slept under a tree all night, it wasn't really sleep. Not the kind that leaves you rested. So, I passed out for the rest of the morning, and never opened my eyes until the heavy scent of supper cooking soaked the air. I smelled some kind of gravy and it roused me from my sleep.

I sat up, dazed and achy, and let my stomach settle before I stepped out of bed. It was a lovely guest room. Ben was right. Freya *was* hospitable. But we were also friends with her brother, the real boss around here. No one really spoke it and I wasn't sure how Finn truly felt about it all.

I found him on the second floor of the Keep.

Staring out a large open window. A few comfortable chairs laid about in front of a few short bookcases. I smiled at the way he'd cleaned himself up since returning home. His usual unkempt red hair now clean, his face not covered in smudges. A tartan still hung across his chest, but a fresh new one instead of the dirty and faded one he used to wear. I wished I could feel the happiness of seeing Finn's face brighten at the sight of me.

"Aye," he said, low and tiredly. "What are ye doin' about?"

"I'm perfectly fine," I lied and forced a smile as I tipped my chin in his direction. "You clean up nicely."

Finn's cheeks reddened, and he beamed with pride as he straightened the pin that held his tartan together. "Aye, well, bein' home… there are certain expectations for me appearance."

I laughed, but it felt hollow in my chest. "You mean people actually expect you to look like a king?"

"A *laird*," he firmly corrected. But there was that familiar grin behind his expression. Then he shook his head as his face turned serious again. "Stop tryin' to distract me." He gently poked me in the arm. "S'what are ye doin' up and about? Shouldn't ye be restin'?"

I shrugged and wrapped the velvet throw I'd taken from my bed tightly around me. There was a chill creeping through my bones ever since I returned from the woods. "I rested enough. I, uh, actually came to ask you for a favor."

Finn's back straightened as he peered down at me dutifully. "What's the matter? The witches nae have news ye wanted?"

I rubbed at my neck. "No. Not really. My only option at this point is to sail down South and find this David Jones guy Ben was talking about."

His forehead wrinkled as his brows pinched together in thought. "But I thought ye couldn't wait that long."

A deep sigh rumbled through me. "I don't have any other options. I refuse to deal with the sirens again. I'm done with the beasts of the sea. I just...I can't."

Finn's shoulders relaxed, and he nodded as he plunked his colossal frame down into one of the chairs. It looked like doll furniture under his massive shape. I took a seat in the other one next to him.

"Aye," he purred softly. "I ken why ye would think that."

I fidgeted with the braided fringe on the blanket. "So, here I am, planning to sail across the ocean once again. And someone once told me you were the best sailing master on the sea."

He waggled his thick red brows and leaned toward me over the arm of his chair. "Ye heard right, then."

Another hollow chuckle turned over in my chest. "So, you'll help me?"

"Was that ever a question in yer mind?" he

replied, feigning offense. "Me feelin's are hurt, Traveller."

Nothing. I felt nothing. Not even when my dearest friend was offering his help, and maybe even risking his life, to help me. I just felt...empty. Cold. Numb. Part of my mind nagged that I should be grateful that I didn't have to endure the pain of being separated from my family with little to no hope of return. But another part screamed that I should be worried that I'd feel nothing ever again.

No. I would. When I got my soul back. Everything would go back to normal. I just had to hold on to that affirmation. For now, I'd cling to the numbness like the drug it was.

I cleared my throat. "How long do you think it will take?"

Finn leaned back and let his wide body completely fill the chair. "I'd have to discuss some things with Benjamin, but I reckon..." he mauled his hand over his neatly trimmed beard. "If we keep to the East, and hit the Southwest current, we could easily make the trip in eight weeks. Ten at the most."

I let that sink in. Ten weeks. I could do that, if I had to, if it were my *only* choice. Which it seemed to be. The choice with less risk, anyway. I could make a deal with the sirens right now; head to the water and ask for their help, beg for my soul back. But what would it cost me? What more could the beasts possibly wish to take from me?

I never wanted to find out.

A groan echoed through me as I pushed off the chair and stood up. I wrapped the blanket snuggly around my back and shoulders before turning to him. "Your sister said we could have a ship."

Finn stared up at me from his chair as the bigger picture of what my words painted registered with him. He nodded dutifully and, in that instant, he was no longer a great laird and I wasn't his guest. No, for a moment in time, we'd unknowingly stepped into our chosen roles, the ones that had once been thrust upon us, but we'd eventually embraced. Right then, in the dimming light of the study, Finn was a sailing master, and I was his captain.

"Aye, I'll ready the ship then." He beamed. "*Captain White.*"

***

After supper, I went back to my room thinking I'd sleep some more, but I only rolled around on the bed in a fit of restlessness. While I felt empty of emotion, the cavity my soul left behind was quickly filling with something else. Something I couldn't quite place. A strange feeling of...I did not know. Not desire. Not need. More of a want, but with no object of interest. Just a thick blanket of the unsatiated craving of the unknown.

When the moon was full and bright in the sky, I huffed an annoyed sigh as I got washed up and threw on my jacket before heading out to walk under the stars. Hoping the cool night air would calm my soulless itch.

My boots padded the damp earth as I wandered about the property. Dragging my fingers across the jagged wood fence. Smoothing a palm over a horse's shiny mane. I kicked at rocks and trailed down the worn dirt path that led me outside the stone wall that surrounded the Keep until I spotted a dark figure stretched out across a large bail of hay.

Lottie.

I strolled over and when her eased state tensed, her head lifted from the hay, I knew she heard me approaching. I smiled and stopped.

"You okay?" I asked.

Lottie let herself relax back on the bail and stared up at the stars above. "Yes, just...thinking."

"Mind if I join you?"

Her answer was a loud pat on the hay by her side. I walked over and sat for a moment before leaning back to lie down. Our arms touched. Only then did I realize how cold I was, when the heat from Lottie's body seeped into mine. I let the sensation soothe me.

The twinkling lights that filled the black sky above shone down and illuminated her pale skin, making it appear like cream as it melded into the blonde waves that sat loosely about her face. Lottie turned her head to face me and eyed me curiously.

"The stars love you," I told her.

Lottie let out an annoyed sound. "What are you

talking about, Dianna?"

I laughed, feeling almost high on the warmth that she'd given me. A sorry substitute for emotion, but it felt good to have something fill the hole in my chest. I nestled closer to her and pointed up at the sky.

"How much do you know about constellations?" I asked.

Lottie's shoulders moved. "I know the North star," she replied. "I'm not sure of the names of any, but my father taught me how to navigate the sea using the shapes. Like that one." She pointed to our left.

I nodded. "Those three right there? That's called Orion's Belt. And those," I added, "are called The Big Dipper. See how it makes the shape of a pot?"

Her twinkling blue eyes stared for a moment before they widened. "What about that one?"

I spent a while just laying with my friend, teaching her all the constellations I knew, enjoying her presence. The comfort she unknowingly offered. She was still clearly weighed down by her immense grief, and rightfully so, but I could see the minuscule signs of her healing. A hint of a smile. The purposeful, deep breaths she took.

When I had no more stars to name, we laid there in silence for a good while. Until the chill of late night crawled over our skin. We never left, though. Only inched closer together. Finally, she spoke.

"You can go now, you know," her voice barely a whisper in the breeze.

"What do you mean?"

"I know you're thinking about staying for me." Her fingers wrapped around my upper arm. "I'll be alright. I'm not quite there, but I will be. Someday." She shifted to look at me and I immediately got sucked into that haunting gaze of blue and silver. "So, you do what you need to do, to get back to Henry and those babies."

The words registered in my mind, but I picked up on something else in her tone and my stomach tightened. "You're not coming, are you?"

She pursed her lips. "I can't, Dianna. The sea..." She stroked a hand over her flat stomach. "It's taken so much from me. I can't bear to sail it again." Lottie sat up then and looked behind us where the massive Keep towered in the shadows. "I think I'll stay on land a while. See if it does me any good."

I took her hand in mine. "I can't blame you. If I get back, I'm not sure I'll ever let the kids near the water again." We squeezed one another's hands and let a look of understanding pass between us. If I could muster it, I'm sure my eyes would have filled with tears. "So, this is actually goodbye then." Lottie only nodded. The tears I wanted to feel myself glistened in her eyes.

"You know," I said, not wanting to leave just yet. "I'd never had friends before."

She reached over and plucked a piece of hay from my hair. "None?"

"Not really." I gnawed at the inside of my cheek.

"After losing my mother, everything else seemed so trivial. So...pointless. I thought, why bother when the potential loss could hurt me so much?" We stared at one another for a few moments. "I'm glad I bothered with you."

A weak attempt at a chuckle died in her throat, but she held a smile.

"I love you, Charlotte Roberts."

Her smile spread wider. "And I love you, Dianna White."

To hear my chosen name spoken in this time brought a tickle to my throat. I no longer wore the burden of the Cobham name. Not in this time or the next. I wanted to feel that emotion, wanted to let it fill my chest with a fiery spark that should spread up to my eyes. But all I had was the rational thought of knowing I would feel it again someday. If I were to succeed in my mission. It gave me a rush of confidence that I could do this, I could sail across the ocean and journey to the Caribbean to save my soul. I could get back to where I belonged.

I just hoped the loss of my emotions wouldn't get in the way.

CHAPTER FIVE

It took Freya and Finn only a few days to ready a ship for us. But it may as well have been a few years for how long it felt to me. Every second that ticked by was a second too long without my family, without knowing what they were doing or thinking. I worried about what Henry might do in my absence. What crazy lengths he might be going through to save me.

But I didn't need to saving. *Except from myself.* I shook the thought from my mind and continued pacing about my room, packing my scarce belongings. I just needed my soul. Once I had that, Ingrid swore the Keepers would send me back.

I'd spent the time waiting by trying to focus

internally, to try and figure out what I'd done under that tree. How I seemed to have just...turned off my emotions. It's not that I felt dead inside, I consciously knew how I *should* feel in any given situation, I just couldn't seem to locate the feeling inside. Almost as if my emotions had been locked in a box somewhere. I tried everything; breathing, meditating, even calling upon old memories I had of the kids. Their birthdays, vacations, their first words. Simple but important moments that should evoke a tear or two.

But I had nothing. Just that dark, insatiable, nagging feeling that pulled me toward something I didn't know. Like being led in the dark, blindfolded.

A knock at the door startled me, but a deep breath and a glance out the window to the carriage below told me it was probably just someone letting me know they were ready to go. I opened the door to find Lottie.

"You ready?" she asked.

I took one more look around my room. "Yeah, I'm ready."

She motioned for me to follow. "I'll walk you out."

We walked in silence through the winding halls of the Artair Keep. I took it all in. The plaques, the medieval art, the oil paintings of Finn's family—especially the ones that had him in it. A young buck. So handsome and proud in every single one. Despite his father's oppressing thumb, Finn somehow stayed true to himself and never let it change him. In a time like this, a world so unforgiving of such things as being gay, it was more than admirable. Had Henry and I chosen to raise the twins in the past, their Uncle Finn would be someone I'd be honoured to have them look up to.

Lottie came to a halt on the wide stone steps out front while I continued down the few short stairs toward the carriage. I turned one last time to look at her and she let a kind smile spread across her face. But her eyes widened as she glanced over her shoulder, something inside the house catching her attention.

By the time she whipped her head back to me, and her mouth gaped urgently, Freya appeared and brushed by Lottie on her way to the carriage. She wore an emerald-coloured cloak over brown leather attire. Hilts of tiny daggers adorned her legs; her waist hugged with a thick belt that held a rather enormous sword at her side. That fiery red hair tied down in a long braid that cascaded all the way down her back. She plunked a leather satchel down near my feet and gave me a cheeky smirk as she stood in wait.

"Are you coming?" I asked and tried not to sound as surprised as I felt.

She straightened those wide shoulders of her and flashed those meadow green eyes. "Who'd ye think was goin' to sail the ship?" Freya fixed her stare on Lottie. "Be sure to keep a close on things." My friend nodded dutifully, but her cheeks reddened when her eyes landed on mine. "Very well." Freya motioned to a young woman I didn't recognize, and the girl came over to fetch the bag at my feet. "Let's get goin'."

I stepped into the carriage after Freya and Finn. Benjamin clambered in behind me, along with three female deckhands. The large carriage sank under all our weight, but when the driver flicked the reins of the horses, I pulled back in my seat and we were off.

With nothing to really say, I stared out the window and let myself get lost in my own thoughts. Freya was going to sail the ship down South. If this were a few years ago, that notion would have ignited some kind of jealous anger in me. Some territorial reaction. But all I had now was my rational mind to depend on, and it told me it was okay. This wasn't my ship, wasn't The Queen. And it wasn't my crew, either. The three deckhands Freya brought along appeared more than able-bodied with their Amazonian heights and toned arms. I knew they could help steer our course. But, again, they weren't my crew. They were Freya's, just as the ship was. I didn't have to captain it at all.

The relief was almost palpable.

The ride to the docks was bumpy and quiet as we all sat and contemplated the next ten weeks of our lives. Ben tried several times to engage me in conversation, but I was all too aware of Freya's watchful eye. So, I kept the chit chat simple and when he realized I wasn't in a talking mood he turned his attention to Freya. She happily lapped it up; laughing at his jokes and touching him any chance she could. His arm, his leg, a pat on his chest.

I just continued to stare out the window and think of Henry and the kids. Painted their faces in my mind, carved out every detail. The sharp line of Henry's pink lips, his rough but gentle hands, and the way they felt against my skin. How the thick blonde hair he kept long would tangle around my fingers when I wrapped my arms around his powerful neck. And the kids...the smell atop their heads, the little pudgy arms holding me while I held them, their smiles, the way those dark eyes—just like their father's—sparkled with childlike wonder.

If this worked, I'd see them soon.

When the carriage finally stopped and we all filed out the small door, I stood and stretched my legs as I took in the sight of everything. The docks lined the small shore of what looked like a narrow inlet. A handful of small fishing vessels bobbed on the surface of the water, while one larger ship sat waiting near the end.

"That's her," Finn spoke as he leaned into me and nudged his shoulder to mine. "Lady Brianna, named after me Ma."

It was a good-looking ship, not as large as The Queen, but more than fit for the wide-open sea. Six portholes lined each side of the vessel made of some kind of warm, rich coloured wood. Two masts towered above, sporting cream-coloured sails. The word Lady Brianna sharpened into view the closer we got, and I stopped at the plank that bridged the gap between the dock and the ship.

The deckhands carried goods onboard and Freya followed them with Ben and Finn in tow. So I trailed after them all as I tugged at the straps of my leather bag. When our modest group of sailors were all standing on the deck, Freya gave the girls some orders before heading off to the captain's quarters, but I caught the cheeky look she flashed toward Benjamin before she entered her room. I rolled my eyes and turned to Finn.

"Can you show me where my bunk is?"

"Of course, lassie," he replied happily and waved me over. "Follow me."

Without prompting, Ben joined us, and we lowered ourselves down a ladder hatch to the decks below until Finn led us to a narrow hall lined with half a dozen doors.

"Here," he pointed for me. "This be yer room. And this one," he smacked his palm against the door next to mine and looked at Ben with a foolish grin, "is yers. I'm goin' t'head up and ready us for push off."

Benjamin nodded gratefully and let his large duffel bag fall from his shoulder as he looked at me, both our hands on the knobs of our doors. We paused and let a strange, unspoken weight pass between us. We knew what was ahead, the dangers and the risks of what we were doing. The sea had never been kind to either of us yet, still, we ran to it. But it was the only way to get my soul back, and we both knew it. We both sucked in a deep breath and then entered our separate bunks without a single word uttered.

My room was small but roomy, with enough space to move around comfortably. My bunk nestled in a built-in wood frame and was dressed in heavy woolen blankets and furs. An empty chest sat open and waiting for me to fill it with my belongings, but I just plopped my bag down inside it before sitting on the edge of the bed. A small table held a washbasin on top and a chamber pot underneath. Was I ready to spend ten weeks stuck inside this room? At least as captain, I would have had duties, responsibilities, something to occupy my mind. If I was going to do this, I was going to need a job.

I left my bunk and headed to the upper deck in search of Freya, hoping she was still in her quarters. I knocked at the thick wooden door and waited for her reply on the other side. When her voice rang out, I entered. She stood behind a beautiful desk carved from the wide trunk of a tree and sat down as she looked up at me.

"Dianna," she said. "I trust yer getting' settled?"

I nodded. "Yes, thanks." I stepped further into the room, noting the elegant draperies around the enormous bed, the stacks of books, the open trunk that sported weapons of all kinds. "I just wanted to ask if there's something I could do aboard the ship while we sail. A job? A regular task?"

Freya eyed me curiously. "What can ye offer?"

"Well, I'm actually a fairly skilled cook."

She nodded slowly. "Yes, that's right. I ken ye like to be in the kitchen." She shuffled some things on her desk. "I dinnae see why not. I'm bettin' yer cooking be better than Aleery's anyway. She favours her plain meat and boiled potatoes. I reckon it's all the lassie can cook."

We both chuckled, but the sound was hollow in my chest. I cleared my throat, unsure what to say next. Freya just stared up at me expectantly.

"Uh, I guess I'll get going then," I said and turned to the door. "Oh, and thank you."

"Fer what?"

"For...everything, I guess," I replied. "For accepting us into your home, helping us when we needed it. And now, providing this ship and transport down South. I'm not sure I can ever repay you."

Freya waved her hand at me and shook her head. "'Tis what decent folk do, is it nae?"

I gave a single shrug and gripped the doorknob. "Still, I'm grateful."

Just as I was about to close the door behind me, she called out. "There is one way."

I came to a halt and backed up into the room. Freya stood from her chair and came around to the front of her desk where she leaned against it. She crossed her arms.

"Anything," I replied.

Her freckles almost disappeared behind the rush of crimson that spread over her cheeks. "I fancy

Benjamin very much."

Unsure where this was going, I shut the door and took a deep breath. "Yes, I'm aware. Ben's a great guy, one of my best friends."

"And I'd very much appreciate it if ye would keep it that way," she told me.

Confused, I stepped closer. "You do know that I'm married, right?"

"Aye," she said and heaved a sigh. "I ken yer married to Captain Barrett. I just wanted to affirm that ye remembered it, too."

What was that supposed to mean? A sting of anger touched the bottom of my gut, but I pushed it aside. I would not fight with this woman about this. Not here, on her ship. "Freya, I'm not sure what you're insinuating, but Ben is one of my closest friends on this earth. And I'm happily married to an amazing man, the same man I'm desperately trying to get back to."

Her chin raised for a moment as she seemed to consider her next words as carefully as I did. Finally, she settled into a mask of a smile. "Of course. I meant nae offense. I just hope to pursue things with Mr. Cook, and I want to make sure the line ye've drawn stays uncrossed." When I didn't reply, she continued. "It's no secret to anyone with a set of eyes that he's madly in love with ye, Dianna. Clearly ye ken that."

My stomach clenched. "Yes, I'm aware. But Ben and I have an understanding. It's what makes our friendship so strong."

"Aye, well." She shoved off the desk and stood, towering over me. But not in an intimidating way. More of a...insecure way. Hidden beneath her powerful will. I wondered then if Freya had ever pursued a man before. "We shall see. Ten weeks is a long trip."

My mouth hung open, ready to counter her worries with more assurances, but the door behind me opened and Finn came stomping in.

"Sorry t'interupt ye," he churred, "But I need a word with me sister before we set course."

I shook my head. "No, it's okay. It's no bother." I caught Freya's eye across the room and held it for a moment. "We're done here."

I felt her eyes on my back as I walked away, even after I shut the door behind me and headed across the deck.

This *was* going to be a long trip.

***

A few days at sea and the hours were already blending together. I kept myself busy during the day, bustling about the generous kitchen. Preparing meals, cleaning, keeping my hands busy. I was grateful for it, for the idle work, just as much as the crew seemed to be grateful for the decent meals I provided.

I considered it all a blessing because at night when I retired to my bunk and succumbed to the drags of sleep, I entered a whole new world. One full of darkened shadows and eerie whispers. This was the fourth night in a row I stood in an empty room. No windows, no doors. No way in or out to speak of. The tendrils of a dream tugged at my subconscious from all around, firmly planting me in the unknown place while I awaited the same nightmare that haunted me each night.

The surrounding air stopped as if frozen in time, and I knew what was about to happen. The same thing that every nightmare had brought me for the last three nights. In the far corner of the room, a cloud of black smoke crept in through the cracks n the wall. Fluid and beautiful, like ink in water. It crawled toward me, screaming silently through the air until it touched my skin and immediately my back arched. The darkness seeped into my pores, leaked into my body, and took residence where my soul used to be. I could feel it swirling around my insides, wreaking havoc on everything. Tearing at the walls of my stomach, squeezing my heart until I gasped for breath. I couldn't move, couldn't cry for help. I knew it was only a dream but, still...fear rose in my chest, igniting the deadened flesh where emotions used to live.

My screams fell on no ears because I was always alone. But this time...I sensed another presence. I peeled my eyes open and squinted through the dark swirls of ink, but found no one. Just the empty room filled with my own screams of agony. But beneath that, the faintest sound of whispers reached my ears, and I embraced the darkness to lesson my cries so I could hear the sound.

She doesn't have a soul...
What a gift...
Live foreeeever...
Pretty little thing...
Forever...

I sucked in a heavy breath with a gasp. The inky smoke burned in my lungs. But it subsided. A door suddenly appeared in the middle of the room, held up by nothing other than the floor it stood from. Frantic and desperate to leave this place, this confusing and haunting nightmare, I flung the door open and thrust myself through the void.

I awoke in my bunk with a fright, fighting for air. But one breath was all I needed. Confused, I sat up in the dim light of my room–the stub of a candle the only light to be found–and held up my hands in front of my face. Calm. Even. I touched my chest. No racing heartbeat. No sweat-covered skin. I was cool as a cucumber.

But how? And better yet...*why*?

I slowly laid back down in bed, knowing very well it was too late in the night to get up and wander about. I was still. Unmoving and bewildered at the dream that seemed to plague me. Why now? Was it the sea working its wild magic on me, or was I just yearning for my family? Perhaps it was my body's way of coping with the loss of my emotions. I felt empty inside, lost at times. But now, as I laid there on the bed, I felt something new. A sort of tugging in my chest, pulling me toward that same darkness that haunted my dreams. As if it were the answer. And for the first time in days, I finally felt the full effect of an emotion.

Fear.

CHAPTER SIX

I went about each day with a routine. I spent as much time as I could in the kitchen. Cooking, cleaning, preparing, baking. Whatever I could to keep my hands busy. Because it helped. To not have idle hands...it just made the nights so much worse. Because at night, I drowned in nightmares. The same ones. Over and over. The darkness just ate at me until there was nothing left but a dried-up shell in the mornings. It took me a solid hour just to get out of bed each morning. But, when I did, the kitchen was there to save me. There was an endless number of chores to do in a kitchen. It was perfect for someone like me. And I eventually found a loophole to avoid the nightmares.

Just stay awake.

The darkness, it couldn't bother me unless I slept. But, after two whole nights of forcing myself awake, I roamed the ship on the third night. Restless. I could feel the drags of sleep pulling at me. I headed up a ladder hatch and walked the upper deck. Let the cool night air fill my lungs. Ignite my senses and keep me awake.

I leaned against the far back railing and stared down at the crashing waves below. They always mesmerized me. Like liquid jade rolling in the night.

*Dianna…*a voice whispered from behind.

I whipped around to find no one, but my heart beat once and hard and it made me stumble back. I gripped the railing and took a deep breath just as Finn appeared. He looked almost as tired as I felt.

"Why am I nae surprised to find ye up here at this hour?" he said, and I turned and leaned against the railing with him.

"I don't know." I shrugged. "What else am I going to do?"

We both stared down at the waves below. A good while passed before either of us spoke and I savoured in the silence. The serenity of just being with one of my closest friends and the sounds of the ship cutting through the ocean. I enjoyed the mutual love-hate relationship he and I shared with the sea.

But, after a while, the silence scratched at my skin. I picked around the edge of a fingernail. "Tell me a story, Finn."

"A story?" he balked.

"Yeah," I said and inhaled a big gulp of sea mist. "Tell me something. Anything."

"What do ye want t'know?"

I thought for a moment. "Why did you choose to leave behind your home again? After waiting so long to get it back."

His forehead pinched together. "Ye asked me to."

I shook my head. "You could have said no."

"Dianna," Finn said, almost scoldingly. "Sometimes...the family ye were born with just drifts away. Just a wee bit." He paused thoughtfully. "Ye still love them. But then the family ye choose for yerself takes a higher place in ye heart." We both leaned against our arms on the railing and looked at one another. "Yer me family, Dianna. Ye and Henry, Lottie...*Gus*."

We took a moment of silence. I hadn't realized how fresh in my mind the death still was. How it all happened. Just a flash of images forever seared into my brain. Black kelpie blood poisoning the water around us. Mixing with the crimson swirls of human blood. The struggle and cries of my friends, of Henry. The gut-wrenching sound of metal hacking through the thick hide of the kelpies. I'd never forget it as long as I lived.

"If yer in need of help, I'll be there in any way I can." His face twisted, and he looked at me from the corner of his eye. "Freya's just a stubborn wench."

I laughed, but it fizzled out and we settled back into a comfortable silence as the crashing jade lulled us. The stars above were so bright, the sky so clear, that I could see everything around us in sharp detail.

After a moment too long, Finn spoke. "Yer worried, aren't ya?"

I just pursed my lips and nodded, keeping my gaze fixed on the water. I knew I should have tears. Knew how I *should* feel inside. But I just felt...cold. Not the kind that left a chill, but a sort of icy caress that combed me over, inside and out. Calm. Unstirred. I only recognized the importance of my mission in my mind.

There was no emotion to speak of that pushed me forward. Only rationality. I had to get back to my family and this would finally be over.

Finn slung a heavy arm over my back and let it settle across my shoulders, weighing me down with unexpected comfort. "We'll figure it out." His words gave little assurance as I recognized a hint of doubt in his tone.

It matched the one that sat in my empty chest.

CHAPTER SEVEN

I don't know at what point I left the deck and ended up in bed, but I awoke the next morning in my bunk. I laid there for a moment, bewildered and disoriented, until I realized what the problem was.

No nightmare.

I must have forced myself awake long enough to avoid actual sleep and just dipped into a temporary coma for a few hours. I stretched my arms high and my spine cracked. I didn't exactly feel rested and refreshed, but I also didn't face the fatigue from a night of horrors. I'd take it.

I flung the blankets off me and got cleaned up.

Just as I was exiting my room, Benjamin's door creaked open and a wave of laughter poured out. He stepped into the hall where I stood, Freya's arms draped around his neck, and when his eyes met mine, the laughter abruptly came to a halt.

"Morning," I said to them both and forced a smile, ignoring the sting of jealousy I suddenly felt. "I would have expected you two to be sleeping up in the captain's quarters."

Ben went wide-eyed. "Oh, we weren't–"

"Aye, but we got caught up in all the stories Benjamin here was tellin' me," Freya cut in. She looked at me, but her arm remained around Ben's neck and her fingers played with his hair.

"Stories?" I asked.

Benjamin's cheeks filled with a soft pink under the dark brown scruff of his facial hair.

"Aye," Freya replied. "From his days as a real pirate. Fascinatin', really." She shrugged nonchalantly. "Before we knew, we'd dozed off, and the sun was coming up."

That sting of jealousy spread in my chest like heartburn. He'd never told me details of his days of piracy. Not anything significant, anyway. I stomped down the sensation. I also didn't spend nights in his bed. Benjamin and I shared a deep, otherworldly friendship. I couldn't let my envy of Freya's connection to him get to me. I wanted Ben to be happy.

Do you really...

The whisper was so loud in my ear that I let out a

slight yelp. When they both gave me a curious look, I put my palm to my chest. "Hiccups."

Freya nodded slowly, her suspicion of me no secret, and she leaned in to place a kiss on Ben's cheek. "Excuse me, I should check in with Finnigan. I'll see ye later?"

"Uh, yes, of course," he replied and watched her trail down the hallway toward a ladder hatch and disappear. When she was out of sight, Ben's eyes landed right on me, his brows raised. "Nothing happened."

His need to assure me gave me a startle, but I played it cool. "That's too bad. Freya's beautiful."

A long sigh left him, and he stuffed his heavily ringed hands in the pockets of his pants. "Yeah, but she's not..."

I dared bring my gaze to his as we took slow steps down the hall. I saw then what filled his mind; a mess of confusion and pain and heartbreak. I wondered what reflected in mine. Emptiness? Darkness? Whatever had taken residence in the hole left behind by my soul. I shook my head.

"Not what?"

He didn't answer.

A tightness pulled at my shoulders. "Well, you're missing out if you don't make a move soon. Freya's a catch."

"A *catch*?"

I laughed, a real one, and I placed a hand over my chest as if I could hold on to it before it seeped from me. "Uh, yes. Sorry, modern term. It means...someone who has it all. Everything you need or are looking for. Beauty, smarts, strength."

We walked a bit more, nearing the ladder hatch that would bring us to the mess deck. He stopped at the bottom and peered down at me with a contemplative expression.

"Would I be considered a...*catch*?"

I pretended to ponder on it for a moment, taunting him, then waggled my hand in the air. Benjamin chuckled and playfully shoved at my arm. I reciprocated the gesture and, when my hand fell to my side, my fingers brushed against his and my heart fluttered. I gasped at the sudden rush in my chest.

"Ben!" Finn called down from above. I glanced up to spot his fiery red hair through the large square opening. "Need ye up here."

Relief flooded me, calming my unpredictable heart. Ben didn't seem to notice the turmoil I battled with inside. He turned back to me and smiled.

"See you later, then?"

I just nodded as he scrambled up the ladder hatch. I headed for the mess hall, all the while thinking about what I'd done. I had no actual explanation, but part of me recognized the fact that I somehow turned off my emotions. Or...most of them, anyway. And they seemed to be replaced with fear and...something else. Lust? No, not quite. Something I just couldn't put my finger on.

I feared that the lack of a soul was changing me,

altering me on a deep level. And I worried if it would revert, even if I got my soul back because I couldn't possibly live the rest of eternity like this. The idea of getting back to my family seemed logical in my mind, but it didn't make my heart flutter. Not like it just did when Ben's hand touched mine, and certainly not like it did when the pang of jealousy ran hot in my veins at the sight of Freya coming out of his room.

What was happening to me?

***

Just a few days later, we made a stop along the way as we hugged the Western shores of France and Spain. Freya called the orders to have the ship anchor by some docks near a village in Portugal. I tried to muster up my pathetic amount of history knowledge from high school. Portugal. Early 1700s. I think it was King Joseph who currently ruled the area, after just making a treaty between Britain and Portugal.

The Lady Brianna anchored just a short way out, and we all clambered into a rowboat to go ashore. Freya muttered something about not wanting to go into port and preferring to avoid dealing with any local pirates that may hustle the visitors. Honestly, I hadn't really been paying attention when she spoke, I was too concerned with getting ashore and away from the ship. Whatever I had done to myself, whatever was going on inside of me...it wracked my nerves, dwindled my emotional range down to a splinter. The world was looking pale and boring. Like a starving animal, I desperately ached for new surroundings to ignite my senses.

Finn took my hand and helped me from the rowboat to the dock and I stood and stretched my back, breathing in deeply the fresh scents, unfamiliar sounds. Things like spices and Earl Grey tea, fresh linens, and fruit all filled my nostrils and my mouth instantly salivated.

The port was bustling with movement all around as the afternoon sun shone down on everything like a shiny golden blanket. Merchant tents and kiosks were spattered across the entire length of the shore as far as I could see. Traders, sellers, locals, and visitors alike filled the space between them all. A quick glance at the tents closest to us told me that there were things like delicious foods to decadent chocolates and even some hand-crafted jewellery. It was certainly a sight to behold and one that wouldn't last long. As I raked through my meager knowledge of the place and time, Portugal would soon fall under a war. A small one, a quick one. But a war, nonetheless. Spain and France would eventually grow leery of Portugal's treaty with Britain and will attempt to take over. They won't win, but I vaguely recalled learning how the beauty of the place would be destroyed for a while. I inhaled deeply, appreciating the fact that I was lucky enough to see it all in its prime when it was bursting with life and cultures mixed beautifully.

"Aye," Freya announced, and we all turned to face her with our bags in hand. "I'll go fetch us some lodgings for the night."

Finn straightened his belt. "And now that I got ye all ashore, I best be headin' back to the ship to finish securin' everythin' and bring the deckhands in."

I slung the strap of my satchel over my head and let it rest against my side as I looked at Benjamin. "Care to check out the market with me?"

"Lead the way," he replied with an eager smile.

I ignored the way Freya stared daggers into me as I turned my back to her and headed toward the never-ending rows of merchants. The food we'd packed aboard The Lady Brianna was great, but my stomach rumbled violently at the sight and smell of the wondrous things at our fingertips. Slow-cooked meats in various sauces, freshly poured chocolates, spicey fish dishes, and more. I got something from just about every food vendor we passed and shared it with Benjamin. He happily lapped jams and sauces from the spoon we shared.

"I swear," Benjamin said, "I'll never grow tired of food."

"Not after a hundred years living off of plain fish and stale bread," I replied with a wicked grin.

He playfully shoved at me and I laughed, a genuine sound that felt heavy in my chest. Soul or not, being with Ben made me feel alive. There was no doubt in my mind about that. I was going to miss him greatly.

I unwrapped the twine that closed some chocolates bound in a meshy fabric and broke a piece off. "Here," I said and put it to his mouth. "Try this."

He waited for a second, laying his eyes on mine and letting his brow lower before his mouth opened enough for me to stick the chocolate on his tongue. As I dragged my hand away, our eyes still locked together, Ben's lips ever so slightly brushed the skin of my fingers and I felt my heart squeeze in my chest. The tip of his warm tongue licked a smear of chocolate from my thumb.

It was a step too far. I knew that the second it happened. But the feeling of Benjamin's lips on me, even my finger, was enough to light my veins on fire and they suddenly burned like gasoline ablaze. I took a step back and focused on a long breath to clear my head as I willed my body to simmer.

Benjamin's mouth opened to speak, but, thankfully, a stark cry for help pierced the air and saved me from having that awkward conversation. Our heads whipped to the left where a small boy, not much older than my own children, was being dragged to the center of the market where a large stump of wood sat. He struggled against the man who gripped his arm tightly, wailing to be let go.

"No, please, sir!" the kid begged. "No!"

"I'll teach you to steal from me, you street trash," the man, clearly a merchant, told him and forced the boy to his knees as the man stretched his tiny arm over the stump.

I noticed then, the darkened and dried stains of reddish-brown soaked into the wood and an axe that sat perched against the side. The merchant held the flailing boy as everyone watched in wait, and he picked up the axe.

I looked at Ben, who was staring at me in dismay. But not at what we were witnessing. He was giving *me* a look of disbelief, as if I'd done something wrong. It was just a fleeting look, but enough to make me question it before he dove for the man and grabbed his arm in mid-swing.

"What do you think you're doing?" the man bellowed, his other hand still gripping the boy's tiny wrist.

"He's just a kid," Ben replied. "What did he steal to warrant losing a hand?"

The boy sobbed helplessly at their feet as the man guffawed. "A loaf of bread."

Ben's eyes widened. "*A loaf of bread?*" His expression intensified with anger and he squeezed the man's arm so tight that the axe fell and rattled to the ground. He gave the merchant a hefty shove, and he stumbled back. "Here," Ben said with a bite and pulled a small pouch of coins from his pocket and tossed it at the man who scrambled to catch it. "This should cover a thousand loaves of bread. If a hungry child comes around, you give them food." He took two wide steps toward the man and let his massive height tower down over him. "Do you understand?"

With a frantic nod, the merchant scuttled away, and I began walking over to where Ben was helping the boy to his feet. He kneeled to face him. "Why were you stealing?"

The kid's sobs had settled into quiet hiccups, and he wiped at his tears with his dirty hand. "My little sister hasn't eaten in days, sir. I was just trying to help her."

"Where are your parents?" Ben asked.

"Dead, sir."

Benjamin ran a hand roughly over his own face and let a deep sigh loosen from his chest with a low grumble. I watched as he reached into his backpack and rifled around until he pulled out another pouch, a larger and lumpier one.

"Here," he said, and handed it to the kid. "This should be more than enough to feed and house you both for the rest of your lives." The boy stared blankly at the bag and then up at Ben. "No more stealing, okay?" The kid nodded as new tears filled his eyes. "And if you see someone else who needs help, you do what you can. You understand?"

Tiny arms flung around Benjamin's neck and the boy thanked him over and over before running off.

"Just giving away all your treasures now, are you?" I said jokingly as Ben stood and faced me.

He brushed some dirt from his pants and gave me another pinched look. "Well, let's just say...the situation hits close to my heart." Those chestnut eyes only continued to dig at me. "Are you alright?"

My shoulders slumped. "Yeah, why wouldn't I be? I wasn't the one getting my hand chopped off." I spun on my heel to head back toward the merchant tents.

"Dianna!" he said with a raspy gasp and clutched my arm to spin me back toward him. I collided with his wide and hard chest and glared up at him. "That was a *child*," he spoke slowly and pointedly. He searched my eyes back and forth as if he could find the answer he needed there. "What's happening to you?"

I ripped my arm away and stepped back as I glowered at him, noting how something was blossoming in my chest. Not a warmth, not a feeling or emotion. But a...darkness. Cold and fluid, filling all the empty cavities left behind by my soul. But my rational mind was still there, and it screamed for me to understand, to see what Ben was talking about. But I simply couldn't bring myself to face it. I felt something chilly and wet film over my eyes. Just for a split second, but it was enough for Ben to catch. He recoiled, but before he had the chance to speak, I turned my back to him and stalked off toward the village to find the tavern Freya booked for us.

I couldn't face him, couldn't face what I knew was happening inside of me. Not yet. If I acknowledged the fact that something was wrong with me, then I'd be giving it power. *More power than it already had.* And I feared it would sway me from my mission to get back home to Henry and the kids.

But, as I put more and more distance between Benjamin and me, something sinister whispered in my ear.

Let me in, Dianna. Let me in and you can staaaayyyy...

CHAPTER EIGHT

I stared into the void before me as I sat and mindlessly pushed around the food on my plate with the back of a fork. Some kind of thick stew on a bed of potatoes. It held no appeal to me, even though I knew I hadn't eaten in hours.

My friends and crew sat around the rather large table we occupied in the dining area of the tavern we were staying at, and their voices were like distant echoes as I sunk further and further into my mind. While most of my emotional range was gone, fear seemed to be one of the few I could hang on to. Fear of not getting home, fear of not having and soul and what that truly meant—what it was doing to me. Fear of that voice, that tempting purr that had taken residence in my mind.

I played it over and over. *Dianna. Dianna. Dianna.* Memorizing the sound of it. Trying to decipher what it was and where it may have come from.

"Dianna!" Finn's voice broke through the fog that surrounded me. A layer of impatience lacing his tone.

I blinked away the film that seemed to cover my eyes and looked at him from across the table. He raised his thick red brows. "What?" I asked.

"I was just sayin' that we leave at first light," he replied hesitantly, and all eyes at the table fell on me with question and concern. "We stocked up on everythin' we needed for the rest of the journey. So, be ready."

I just nodded and focused on pushing my food around some more. From the corner of my eye, I spotted Freya shift in her seat and lean toward Benjamin where she wrapped her hand around his forearm. They shared a quiet laugh and jealousy blossomed in my chest. The only other actual emotion I seemed to be able to muster since I flicked that switch inside of me.

I let out a groan and set my fork down before shoving my chair out.

"Are ye leaving?" Freya asked. "Ye haven't even touched yer food."

I gave an impatient shrug. "I'm not

feeling...hungry." *Or anything at all.* "I think...I'll take a walk."

Ben and Finn's voices mixed as they clashed against my back. I ignored them and headed for the door. Night had fallen a while ago, and a thick blanket of black stretched overhead like a canopy. I strolled along the side of the dirt roads that wound in and around stores, houses, and other structures.

I'd no idea how long I'd wandered when I emerged to an open area filled with locals around a large fire pit. A pig roasted and turned over on a spit. A few of the same vendors I saw in the market were there with smaller tables of food they were serving. Someone played a strange-looking guitar, fat and round in shape, but it churned out a lovely upbeat tune that seemed to ignite cheer in the people.

Hunger had no place in my stomach, but my logical mind knew I should eat something. I may be immortal, but I wasn't indestructible. Hunger could still kill me. So, I waited in line at one of the tables and paid for a small bowl of some kind of spicy seafood dish and a large piece of buttered bread. I found a spot to sit on a makeshift bench made from a log and picked at the food. My mouth salivated at the first bite and I knew then, just how hungry I must have been.

I sat until my bowl was empty, let the warmth of the fire soak into my chilly skin, and tried to enjoy the lovely music that danced in the air. I watched as children stuffed their faces and played in the dirt, happy and carefree, and thoughts of my own children rattled in the back of my mind. I missed them, I knew that, but nothing changed in my chest at the memory of them. Nothing stirred in my heart. *A blessing and a curse*. I wondered then if it would always be that way if I remained soulless. Cold and empty, unyielding.

No, I had to hold on to the hope that, even without a soul, I would one day figure out how to flip that switch back. To turn my humanity back on and let my full range of emotions fill me. I had to. The idea of coasting through an immortal existence this way...

"Diabo!" some woman cried out in a hoarse shriek. I glanced up to find her, an older lady with grey hair tucked back in a messy bun, pointing at me with a face full of fear. "Diabo!" she yelled again and stomped around the curve of the fire to job her finger in my face. I just sat there, at a loss of what was happening. *"Diabo! Diabo! O diabo mora em você!"*

The music stopped, and people stared. Some with confused expressions, others with just as much gusto and fear as the old woman offered.

"I-I'm sorry," I said and shook my head. "I don't know what you're saying."

"Diabo! Diabo! O diabo mora em você!" she practically spat.

To my relief, a younger lady appeared and gripped the woman's shoulders gently, pulling her away from me. "Mamãe é hora de ir para casa."

She ushered the crazed woman over to a man who took her away toward the village. The younger lady came back to me. "I am so sorry," she said. Her English was impressive. "That's my grandmother. She's...not well in the mind."

Still a bit stunned, I set my empty bowl on the bench I sat on and stood to face her. "It's alright. She just startled me, is all."

The woman was a natural beauty. Her dark hair long and silky, brown eyes that caught the fire perfectly. She stuck out a hand. "Amelia."

I shook it with a smile. "Dianna."

"Well, Dianna," Amelia said. "I hope you enjoy the rest of your evening."

She turned to leave, and words bubbled up from my throat. "What did she mean?" Amelia spun around, her brows pinching together. "Your grandmother. She said *Diabo* when she pointed at me. What does that mean?"

She heaved a sigh, and I caught a slight eye roll. This must have been a regular thing. "It means...devil. But, please, do not let it bother you. Mamãe thinks any woman who wears pants is an abomination."

She laughed, and I mimicked the sound, but it felt wrong in my body. I pursed my lips. "What...what did the other words mean?"

"Other words?"

"Yes, she said," I paused to remember how it sounded. "Something like...*O diabo mora em você? Sorry, I don't speak Portuguese."

Amelia's head tipped back a bit as she realized. "It roughly translates to *the devil lives inside you*." She laughed again. "But, truly, do not let it bother you. She's not been of right mind for years now."

Don't let it bother me? One of the lingering emotions, fear, possessed my body and I stood frozen in place. My feet felt like boulders in the dirt. But I managed a weak smile and a nod for Amelia. "Thank you. I'll...I have to get going now."

She said her goodbyes and trotted off to join the people she'd been hanging out with before her grandmother spotted me. I left and headed toward the beach. The warmth of the fire seeped from my back with every step I took, leaving nothing but a sharp chill to cover my skin. Amelia's grandmother's voice still screamed in my ears, though. As if she stood right next to me.

Diabo!

Every syllable cut deep into my mind because some part of me recognized the truth in it. The devil lives inside of you. Something sinister had definitely taken residence where my soul used to be.

I just wondered how long I could keep it at bay before it filled every empty inch of me.

When I finally reached the empty beach, I stopped for a moment to remove my boots and socks. I carried them in my hand as I strolled along the edge of the sea, let the soft sand caress my bare feet, relished in the way my toes sunk into it.

I couldn't go back to the tavern. Not yet. I was

too afraid to sleep, and I feared what that old woman said would seep into my nightmare and make it even worse. If that were even possible.

I strolled up and down for hours. Until the deep chill of late-night trickled into my bones. But I still wasn't ready to return. I tossed my boots down and plunked myself onto the beach to stare out across the ocean. Beauty and rage intertwined as one. As much as the sea gave, it took two-fold. But, like a wild animal, you couldn't blame it for its nature.

Just then, something moved on the waves. A formless body, familiar and unwanted. My stomach immediately churned at the sight of a siren solidifying before my eyes. Just a few feet from the shore where I sat.

"What do you want?" I spat.

"Curious," the beast replied with a voice layered in a musical tone, sharp like chimes.

"What are you talking about?" I asked, already impatient.

The siren floated closer and more of its form emerged from the gently lapping waves. "Why you haven't come begging for the return of your soul."

A guffaw rolled over in my throat. "Are you saying your kind will just give it back?"

A chilling, high-pitched laugh filled the air around me. "We do not give or take without cost."

"So, that's a no, then?" I barked impatiently. "And you wonder why I haven't come to you? I'd rather spend weeks sailing across the ocean on the slim chance that I could get my soul back rather than even think about lowering myself to asking *you*." I narrowed my eyes at the creature. "I just want to go home. No strings, no conditions, *no* bargains."

The siren went quiet and sunk below the surface of the water. I waited a moment for it to return but, when it didn't, I grabbed my boots and began shoving them on.

"I may be able to help you, Dianna Cobham," the siren spoke as it appeared again, this time a little further out. "If you come into the water."

I shoved on my other boot and stood up, wiping the sand from my pants. "Nice try, but I'm not an idiot."

I wouldn't dare step into the water with the beast. No one in their right mind ever should. They were known for drowning innocents and taking lives. Just as the kelpies did. But that eerie voice suddenly whispered in my ear, taunting.

Do it, Dianna. Go into the water...

As if with a mind of its own, my hand twitched and discreetly moved to hover over the dagger I kept at my side. My sister's dagger. And an idea blossomed in the back of my mind. A dark idea, and one not of my own making. The entity toiling around inside of me pulled at my will with puppet strings and, in that moment, I wanted nothing more than to obey.

I took slow and careful steps toward the foamy edge of the sea and stopped when the toes of my boots dipped under the water.

"That's right," the siren cooed. "Come to me and I'll show you how you can release yourself from this torment." From where I stood, I could see its terrifying toothy grin flashing in the moonlight.

The fingers that still hovered over my dagger were cold and tingly, and animated by another will. My heart raced at the idea, coaxing me forward, inching me closer to the sea creature. I stopped at arm's reach.

"You can make it go away?" I asked as innocently as I could muster. "You can take it?"

The siren nodded as it grinned devilishly. "Yesss...I can take all your pain."

My one hand whipped outward, so fast it startled even me, and my fingers wrapped around the beast's neck. Her eyes went wide in horror, black and glassy. They reflected the full moon above, and in them I saw her fear. The thing inside of me fed on it.

In another flash, too fast to catch, my other hand plucked the dagger from my belt. I squeezed the siren's neck until a gurgled cough choked from her and I pulled her face close to mine.

"Then here you go," I spat. "Take it!"

The blade cut through her watery chest with ease until it reached the spot I was hoping for. Her heart. When a piercing *tink* of metal on stone chimed in the air, I knew I had succeeded. I gave the dagger a good twist, and the siren cried out in pain, a loud ear-shattering wail. Inky blood seeped from the wound and I held her tightly, desperately, the dagger still lodged in her chest, until I watched the eternal life drain from those black eyes.

The knife receded with a wet sound and I returned it to its hilt, not even bothering to wipe the blood from it. I was covered in the stuff, anyway. When I released her body, it returned to the sea in a watery form until it dissipated, and I turned to leave, satisfied with what I'd done. My heart pounded with adrenaline; fat and happy. Wanting more.

When I stepped onto the sand, I stopped for a moment to take a deep breath and let the rush of what I'd done settle over me. I shivered, unable to keep the chattering of my teeth and body at bay. So, I walked mindlessly, wandering through the sleeping town. Unsure of what to do. I couldn't waltz into the tavern covered in blood and soaked to the bone. But I couldn't stay outside, either. I'd surely freeze to death as the night progressed.

I wasn't sure how long had passed when I heard my name called in the distance. Too disoriented and lost in my own mind to see where the sound was coming from, I just stopped in place and waited. My body trembled even more until my stomach began to hurt.

Suddenly, hands were on me, pawing at my arms and cupping my face with warmth, forcing me to meet their eyes.

"Dianna," Benjamin said, this time cutting through the fog I wandered in. "Christ! Dianna, are you alright?"

The last of the darkness that had seemed to animate my body disappeared, and all that was left was me. Cold, empty, trembling with fear over what I'd done. And what I may do again.

"B-Ben?" I managed to get out over chattering lips. My eyes met his, and I felt them water over.

His hands squeezed my upper arms as he held me away from him and took in the full sight of me. He pinched the blood-covered sleeve of my jacket in his fingers and gave me a horrified look.

"It's...not mine," I assured him.

"Whose is it, then?" he demanded.

With no other emotions to water it down, fear possessed me and scrambled my thoughts. "A siren's."

"Did it attack you? Are you hurt?"

I could only nod as I stared blankly over his shoulder. Perfectly fine with the lie. It hadn't attacked me—it was probably planning to kill me, but I hadn't given it the chance.

Benjamin shrugged out of his long brown trench coat and slung it over my trembling body. The fur-lined collar caressed my face, and I sunk into it. Absorbing the familiar scent of musk and spice.

"Let's get you inside and cleaned up," he said, glancing around before leading me back to the tavern.

It felt like only seconds had passed when Benjamin swung open the hefty wooden door to the tavern and led me upstairs to my room. We stopped just outside my closed door and I looked at his face for the first time.

"C-can you–" Confusion swirled in my mind. "I...don't want to be alone."

He let a deep sigh loosen through his nostrils as he seemed to contemplate what I was saying. His massive hand spread over my back comfortingly and he smiled, but one that didn't meet his eyes.

"Sure," Benjamin replied, low and raspy. "I'll stay as long as you need."

My shaky hand twisted the old brass knob and pushed the door open. My room, left unattended all day, sat in chilly darkness and Ben immediately went to the hearth to get a fire started. I stood in the middle of the room, bundled in his coat, unsure of what to do. All I could think of was getting warm.

He got the fire going in no time and came to me to remove the heavy jacket. He slung it over the back of a chair and turned to take in the full sight of me.

"What the hell happened, Dianna?"

"I told you. The siren, it–"

"Attacked you," he cut in impatiently. "Yeah, I get it. But why? How? What were you doing in the ocean to begin with?" His eyes widened. "At this ungodly hour?"

I wrapped my stiff arms around my torso. "I-I don't know." The words were a whisper. "I went for a walk...and the siren appeared, promising it could fix me."

"And you *believed* it?"

I looked away shamefully and shrugged out of my blood-covered jacket. "Obviously not." I held the garment in my quaking hands and stared at the bloodstains.

"Christ," he said and stalked over to me. "Here, let me take that."

He tossed it in a heap on the floor and stood hovering over me. The warmth of his body radiated outward and I all but lapped it up. He bent down and his ringed fingers gently pulled and peeled my soggy boots from my bare feet. Then he stood and looked me in the face. His brown messy hair falling around his cheeks like a curtain.

A smile tugged at the corner of his mouth. "This feels oddly familiar. Do you remember?"

I nodded. "Aboard The Black Soul."

His eyes trailed to the curve of my neck and shoulder where my sister had hacked a sword into my flesh. An icy chill scraped my spine at the memory. Benjamin's finger tugged at the collar of my shirt and pulled it down enough to see the bumpy scar that would forever be there. He groaned at the sight of it.

"What's the matter?" I asked.

"Just making sure it's still you," he admitted, but finished it with a low chuckle.

The fire crackled and filled the room with a lovely warmth. Or was it the nearness of Benjamin that I felt? Regardless, my heart sped up, and I slowly leaned toward him.

A breath away, he whispered, "You should probably get out of those wet clothes."

I cupped my hand over his where it still lingered on my shoulder and stared up into his eyes. Yearning, desire, and a flicker of pain met my gaze, and I wanted nothing more than to take it all away. To give him what he so desperately wanted because...I wanted it, too. I wanted to give in to the attraction we felt for one another, cast aside the world, and forget everything else. Somewhere in the back of my rational mind, or what remained of it, a thought bounced around. I didn't love Benjamin. Not like that. Not like...*Henry*.

My chest tightened and a familiar voice echoed in my ear. *Do it, give in to temptation...*

His hand caressed the skin of my neck, arousing goosebumps over every inch of me until his palm cupped my face and I leaned into it. Soaking up as much of his touch as I could. My fingers, suddenly steady and able, touched his chest and I felt his heartbeat raging beneath the surface. I tipped my head upward, our eyes locking with a fiery intensity, and parted my lips. Waiting. Wanting. Inviting him to take the one thing he wanted.

His face came closer, leaning in and inching his lips dangerously near. But, when Benjamin's mouth was a hair from mine, he tipped his chin down and touched his forehead to mine as he released a long sigh.

"I should probably go," he struggled to say.

I balled the loose fabric of his shirt in my hands.

"No, please," I said, the words a gentle sound that fell to his chest. "I don't want to be alone."

He waited a beat before stepping back, torture smeared across his pained expression. "I think...for both our sakes, being alone is the best thing for you right now. When you're—"

"When I'm what?" I bit. Anger suddenly seethed in my veins. But it wasn't mine. The darkness that now lived in me raged for what it wanted.

"Vulnerable," he replied and scooped his jacket from the chair.

He swung the door open and gave me one last look, as if second-guessing himself, and shook his head before closing the door behind him. I stood in the middle of the room; my damp clothes clinging to my skin that now raced with an itch I couldn't scratch.

What was I doing?

I heaved for breath and doubled over as I braced myself with the foot of the bed. Each breath cleared away the clutter from my mind. Did having no soul also mean I was a murderer *and* a whore? How could I live with myself if Benjamin wasn't as strong as he was and had given in to me? To betray Henry that way. The love we shared, the life we'd built. Whether I ever found my way back to him or not, I still belonged to him. After all he and I had been through, to be with another man—Benjamin of all people—would be the ultimate betrayal.

The weight of my actions, not just with Benjamin...but with the siren, too, came crashing down on me and I slunk to the floor in a heap of fear. I wanted to cry, I wanted to feel everything my rational mind knew I *should* feel. But I was empty. An echo of who I used to be. And I wasn't sure I could ever go back to that version of myself. But, as the heat of desire still crawled over my skin...

...I wasn't sure I even wanted to.

CHAPTER NINE

It was unnerving how small a ship could feel when you confined yourself to just two areas. A few weeks had gone by since we left Portugal and my days on the sea were made of nightmares, the four walls of my bunk, and the relief the kitchen offered my idle hands. It all blended together with the fog of sleep deprivation as I forced myself awake for days on end before crashing. But I had to avoid the crew at all costs. I wasn't sure what was happening inside of me, wasn't certain what I'd done to myself under that tree back in Scotland. But I was seeing the proof of what this new me was capable of, and I couldn't risk being around anyone.

It didn't keep them away, though.

I was elbows deep in dishwater when Finn walked into the kitchen and pulled up a stool to the large table I used as a prep surface. He sat in silence, which was always strange for him. Clearly, he wanted me to speak first.

I bent down to fetch a tray of buns from the oven, purposely not looking at him. "If you're here for the buns, they're too hot to eat."

"I'm nae here fer the buns, lassie," he mumbled. I looked at him then. His green eyes sparkled with worry.

I kept a straight face. "Then what are you here for?"

He tipped his head to the side and studied me. "Dianna. Ye cannae ignore yer feelings over the loss of yer family. It's nae healthy."

"I'm not ignoring my feelings," I said through gritted teeth. *I hardly* had *any to ignore.* "I'm just...I have to keep my hands and mind busy." It wasn't an outright lie, I truly enjoyed the blissful, mindless work of being in the kitchen. It helped me forget about my situation, even for a moment.

Finn nodded. "Aye, I understand. 'Tis easier to put it from yer mind." I just kept working and moving things around on the counter. "But ye cannae forget those who *are* here." Our eyes met. "Those of us who chose t'help ye. Dinnae shut us out."

I set a large copper pot down with a bit more force than needed, and he leaned back on the stool. "Did Benjamin send you to talk to me?"

The skin between his bushy red brows pinched. "Ben? Nae, the lad's been just as quiet and distant as ye. I'm here because I love ye, Dianna. I care fer yer well bein' and I ken how hard this must be fer ye, being away from Henry and the wee ones."

My dry eyes stung with what should have been tears. Instead, they strained behind the void of emotion. The parched prickle an uncomfortable reminder of what I'd done to myself.

"If there were a way I could go home this very second, I would take it," I told him. "But it's going to be a long time before I even see the possibility of that chance. So, this is how I cope. This is how I choose to handle my pain."

Finn rubbed a hand over his beard and eyed the tray of buns cooling off to the side. I rolled my eyes and handed him one, the steam almost scorching the skin of my fingers. He tore it open and let it cool in his hands.

"But there is a way," he said cautiously. "T'go home sooner. Today, even. If ye wanted."

"How—" I narrowed my eyes as the realization struck me. "No. Absolutely not."

He stood from his stool and circled the table to stand near me. "But if they can help—"

"No." I glared up at him. "I will *not* ask the sirens for help. They don't freely give it, not without cost. And I won't put my children in danger ever again. I will find my way home myself, or I won't go home at all."

He seemed taken aback. "But the wee ones..."

"Are perfectly safe at home with their father and grandmother," I said with finality. But he looked pained, saddened at my curt choice of words. I let a slow sigh loosen from my chest. "I appreciate your worry for me, Finn. I really do. But you have to see why I can't crawl back to them. I can't make another deal with the sea Fae. Look at all it's done. Look how it's affected my family. How it nearly took the life of my children." I patted his arm. "I understand that it's the easy way out. I sure I could call them right now and make a deal and be home in time for supper. But I can't do that. I *have* to break the cycle that my mother started so many years ago."

"Aye," he whispered with a nod. "I ken what ye sayin'. I just hate seein' ye like this."

I managed a smile. "I'm fine. I promise." I handed him another bun and his face lit up with glee. "Even better once we've had a good meal."

He took the baked good and shoved the entire thing in his mouth before stuffing it to the side. "Can I help?"

"If you want..." I pointed at the big pot of soup I'd been brewing all morning. "You can take that out. I'll bring the bowls."

"Are ye goin' t'eat with us today?" he asked as he picked up the steaming pot with ease. It looked a normal size in his beastly arms.

I nodded and began stacking a set of bowls and spoons in my hands. "Sure, why not?"

I guess they had noted my absence. It had just

been easier to eat in the kitchen by myself and avoid everyone. Or not eat at all. Hunger still hadn't returned since we left Scotland, and I was relying on my rational mind to tell me when I should eat.

But really...I'd been avoiding Benjamin. If I could feel embarrassment at all, I'd surely be permanently smeared with a flush of red in my cheeks over what had unfolded in my room that night. I thought about it every minute since it happened. The way my body felt, the way it screamed for his touch, his warmth. Shame pounded around in my mind, but my chest echoed like a hollow chamber. And for that, I was grateful.

I felt the crew's eyes on me as I entered the mess hall and set down the dishware. I said nothing, as did they, while I ladled soup into the bowls and handed them out. Ben was last. He sat at the far end of the long rectangular table, and I dared let my eyes flicker to his as my leg faintly brushed his. A rush of heat flared up through my body from the site of contact, and my breath hitched in my chest. We exchanged no words, and no one seemed to notice the split-second touch. No one except for Freya, who eyed me curiously as I stalked over to my own seat at the farthest end of the table.

A murmur of chit-chat sparked up among the crew as they ate, and the room warmed with the afternoon sun that poured in through the porthole windows.

I plunked down on the bench seat and set my

attention on my bowl of soup. The steam that wafted up to my face, the glorious scent of stewed meat and hearty root veggies. I struggled to maintain my focus because, through the layers of conversation over the table, I could feel Ben's eyes staring at me. I moved my soup around in the bowl with a spoon and chewed at the inside of my mouth, straining not to look. Willing myself not to raise my eyes and confirm what I felt.

But I was weak.

I lifted my head and let my eyes slowly trail across the length of the table until I got to the end and crawled my gaze upward to meet his. Two warm brown eyes screamed at me, filled with questions and yearning. We hadn't spoken since that night in my room at the tavern, and I could see now how it tormented him. His bowl sat untouched, just like mine, his spoon not even in his hand.

I watched his mouth move, not with words but with a slow pursing, and then his tongue swiped across his bottom lip. My heart sputtered anxiously, and I gripped the metal spoon until it began to bend in my fingers. The dormant darkness that lurked in my chest sprang to life and clawed at my insides, wanting him. Urging me forward and burying my will.

My lips parted and a fiery breath of air seeped out as a tickle scoured up my spine, and I struggled to remain still in my seat. Across the table, Benjamin lowered his chin and stared at me from beneath a furrowed brow. Want and warning conflicted over his expression.

In one swift movement, he shoved off his chair and bolted to his feet, eliciting a stark yelp from me. The casual conversations that had been exchanging over the table came to a stop and everyone looked toward Benjamin.

"Excuse me," he said gruffly and stalked off toward the exit.

Freya darted off behind him and I remained in my seat. Everyone else glanced around with puzzled faces, unaware of the silent exchange that had taken place between Ben and me. I kept a straight face, attempted to appear just as bewildered as them. But, in my lap beneath the table, the spoon broke in half.

CHAPTER TEN

When I finally heard the roar of Finn's deep voice ringing out across the ship, alerting the crew that we were making landfall, I let out a breath that had holed up in my chest for weeks. I made it. The Caribbean. I managed to sail across the Atlantic once again, unscathed—for the most part—and would soon be on my way to getting my soul back. But most importantly, I managed to avoid Benjamin since leaving Portugal. Which, now given the time to dwell on my actions, was probably the best for both of us. I longed to see something else besides the confines of my bunk and the kitchen where I found refuge.

Noise clamoured in my ears as the crew readied the ship, and we all lowered into a rowboat to get ashore. The Lady Brianna was too large to enter the shallows of the port. I secured my heavy satchel around my body and grabbed an oar to help row us all ashore. The deckhands didn't want to stay behind and wait for Finn this time, so we'd all piled in the small boat and I was thankful Benjamin sat at the furthest end from me.

The darkness that toiled in my chest seemed to have subsided over the weeks that passed, but I recognized a trigger. One of the few things that seemed to rouse it from its unnerving slumber. Benjamin. Or...proximity to him. His touch, his warmth, the sound of his voice. The darkness wanted him and...it toyed with my will.

Rather than enter the bustling port, Benjamin steered us off to the side where we pulled the boat in over a small beach. He tied the rope to a tree and turned to us.

"It's best we don't make our arrival known," he warned.

"Would we nae be welcome?" Finn asked.

Ben threw a glance over his own shoulder toward the port in the short distance, then leaned in and lowered his voice. "This is a hub for pirates from all over the world. They'll spot our ship in the distance soon enough but, for now, we should keep a low profile. Blend in. You just don't know the types you'll run into here." For the first time in weeks, his eyes met mine. "The civil ways of the world don't exactly apply to this place. It's a pirate's world."

I tugged at the taut strap of my shoulder bag. "Well, it's been a while since you were last here. Maybe things have changed."

He stared at me for a moment, his face unreadable. "Maybe."

"Well," Freya spoke up and stuck her arm around Ben's. "Let's go find us a place to stay."

Everyone turned and followed the two of them and I stomped behind in a huff, jealousy suddenly burning in my chest at the sight of her touching Benjamin. By the time we all trudged across the soft warm sand of the beach that stretched the entire length of the pirate hub, I could practically taste the envy on my tongue. It was all I could stand.

The port bustled with people. Pirates and locals and merchants alike. Ships were being unloaded, goods moved about, music played somewhere in the distance. Voices of all volumes rang together and mixed with the heavy scent of various foods cooking in the air. Freya's loud and purposeful laugh pierced through everything as she continued to walk arm in arm with Benjamin a few feet ahead. I stifled an eye roll and averted my attention to the busy alley of shop fronts and what appeared to be apartments of some kind. The ground beneath us was paved with flat stones that were painted a gorgeous teal. The paint had worn through in some areas of high traffic and gave it a sort of rustic look. A beautiful woman with a white feathered robe leaned against the railing of a tiny balcony and peered down at us with a bewitching look. Her glossy blonde hair draped down across her half-exposed bosom.

We entered the building I assumed was apartments but were clearly lodgings. The interior was dimly lit by the bit of sunlight that managed to filter in through closed drapes. Cigar smoke danced in the air as men and women alike sat around in large, comfy chairs. A gorgeous woman on their laps.

I stepped up to Ben's side and tugged at his sleeve. "This is a brothel."

He chuckled lightly. "You won't find a tavern or inn around here, Dianna." When I looked at his face, his eyes were lingering on my lips but quickly averted when a woman appeared and cleared her throat.

"Welcome," she said in a velvety voice. She was beautiful under the years of her lifestyle. Her dark hair, touched with grey, was neatly kept in a loose bun. Her dainty hands clasped in front of her under a thin silky blouse. "What can I do for you?"

"We're hoping you have some rooms available," Benjamin replied. "We're stopping over on our way to the mainland."

Her perfectly penciled eyebrow arched.

"Pirates?"

He shook his head. "No, Ma'am. Just...travellers."

"How many nights?" The woman's chin tipped upward, her deep blue eyes judging us.

Ben looked at me, but I shrugged. I had no idea how long it would take to locate Davy Jones. He gave his attention back to the woman. "Two nights should suffice."

Two? That was it? Was he that confident in his plan? The idea that I could be home with Henry and the kids in a matter of days made my head spin. It did nothing for the useless organ in my chest, however. My eyes averted to Freya's ever-tightening grip around Benjamin's arm, and I grumbled under my breath.

"I'm going for a walk," I told them and bolted for the door before anyone could respond.

I strolled through stone-paved streets and admired the beauty of the eclectic designs. One building adorned with gothic carvings and details painted with gold, while the next showed strength, built of wood and stained dark to contrast with the luscious treasures from the sea. Shells and pearls and gems of all sorts. One section of the narrow alley area consisted of fabric canopies propped up with rustic logs. Under them, an array of tables filled with goods I assumed were brought in by the high traffic of pirates.

I approached one of the tables and ran my fingers over the display of jewelled brooches, rings, and necklaces. Surely far too grand for commoners. The goods were clearly stolen from royal ships and fleets. I stopped and glanced around at the other tables, noting the other goods definitely meant for a higher class. Pearl necklaces, silk fabrics, bags of herbs and spices, coffees, teas, fine china. The stolen goods were endless.

Then it wouldn't matter if you stole some...

A yelp chirped from my throat and I looked around frantically to ensure I hadn't attracted attention. The eerie whisper had been so quiet for so long that I almost forgot what it sounded like. Of course, it would rear its ugly head now. When the temptation of evil was at my fingertips. I wanted to ignore it, but I found my hand skimming over items, touching slick jewels, and smoothing over fabrics. A trader clad in leather gear eyed me and I smiled at him. When he seemed confident I wasn't going to steal anything, he turned his attention to something behind him and I swiftly pocketed a comb carved of bone.

"So, you're a thief now, are you?" a deep, raspy voice purred in my ear.

With a startle, I spun around to come face to face with Ben. His nose just inches from mine. He stared at me with an unreadable expression and my heart bounced around in my chest like a caged animal.

I failed to put away the devilish grin that I felt pinching at the corner of my mouth. "Following me again?"

His suspicious eyes locked on mine and he pursed his lips under the dark scruff that covered his face. I itched to reach out and caress it.

"Just making sure you're not off murdering more mythical creatures," he replied, his tone flat.

I waggled my fingers. "Nope, just common thievery." Benjamin tipped his head and sighed. With an exaggerated eye roll, I fetched the comb from my pocket and put it back. "Happy?"

"Ecstatic," he replied curtly and tugged at my arm to haul me off to the side. He took stock of our surroundings and when no one was in earshot, he leaned toward me. "I actually thought you'd like to go see David Jones."

"Already?"

"Well, there's something we have to go do first." His shoulders shrugged dramatically. "Unless you'd like to wait?"

"No, no," I hastily replied. "Where do we have to go?"

Benjamin pressed his lips together and craned his neck to throw his gaze out toward the sea in the far distance. "Somewhere I haven't been in a lifetime or two." He breathed deeply. "Home."

***

I followed Benjamin for nearly half an hour before we came upon a small, rundown village further inland. There were no merchants, no shops, not even a house to be found. Just tiny huts that were thrown together with debris and other things. I noted how there was hardly an adult to be seen, and children littered the dirt-clad street that ran down the middle. Soiled rags hung from their skinny bodies. Some played, while others sat around and glared at us as we passed. One child, not much older than ten, sat perched on a log and carved a piece of wood in his little hands with a concerning blade.

That's who Ben approached. "Boy," he said and nodded his chin. "Who is the marketeer here?"

"Dannon," the kid replied with an accent I couldn't quite place, and he pointed to a beautiful home in the distance.

Ben looked at me and cocked his head toward the property before heading off. I scrambled behind him.

"What is this place?" I asked him.

He didn't break his stride. "This is where I grew up, Dianna."

"What?" I looked around, seeing the area differently as I tried to picture a little Benjamin running around in rags. "Were you born here? Where were your parents?"

He waited a moment before answering. "I don't remember them. I was hardly four years old when a crew of slave traders plucked Abraham and me from our home and brought us here." He clucked his tongue. "I didn't expect it to be exactly the same. After all these years, they're still ripping children from their mothers and forcing them into slavery."

"You were...a slave?" The words were bitter in my

throat.

"A pearl harvester, to be more precise," he replied. "One of the neighbouring islands was once lush with beds of shelled sea life. I spent every day for years, diving and swimming around the rocky shores. We weren't allowed to return until our bags were full."

I knew he was from the Caribbean, but that was about all I knew of his past. He continued walking, but I grabbed his arm and forced him to face me. "Ben, you were an orphan *and* a slave?" I shook my head. "Why didn't you ever tell me?"

He shrugged away from my touch. "You never asked."

We stood in place for what felt like eons, just locked in an embracing stare as our chest slightly heaved with the labour of walking and the intensity that seemed to swarm around us.

"Look, are we...going to talk about what happened—"

His hand whipped up and waved off my words. "No need," he blurted. "I get it. You're lost in the past, away from the one you love, torn away from your children." A dry swallow worked its way down his thick throat, and I could see in his brown eyes how he struggled to believe his own words. "You're lonely and confused—"

"Let's just get this over with." I sucked in a deep breath, but it fettered in my chest as I stalked past him.

He jogged to catch up with me and fell in stride

by my side. "Sorry," he said glumly. "I know you don't like to talk about them. I can't imagine how hard it is."

"Tell me more about your life here," I changed the subject, hoping he'd catch on. "How long did you live here?"

He thought for a moment. "I believe I was about fifteen, maybe a little younger, when a crew of pirates came into the port looking to recruit. Abraham brought me with him, lied about my age, and that was the last time I ever saw this place."

We came to a halt just outside an old iron gate. It surrounded the grand home the boy had pointed to, and I peered in through the bars to examine the property. Once lush gardens now overgrown with weeds and deadened leaves. Ivy crawled over the stone figures of lions that sat perched on either side of the stairs that led to the entrance. The home, clearly an old mansion, was three stories tall and some windows in the higher level were boarded up.

"It doesn't look like anyone lives here," I noted.

Benjamin stared at the mansion with a pained and distant expression. "No, he's there." He turned and pointed back to where we came from. "Or *they* wouldn't be."

Without another word, he pushed open the gate and the sound of metal on metal screeched through the air. A flock of birds took off from one of the overgrown trees near the side of the property, and we continued toward the wide stone staircase. I followed behind him quietly as he turned the giant brass knob and hauled open the door. I found it strange that there were no guards, no locks on anything. Anyone could just stroll on into this marketeer's mansion? A man who wrangled child slaves and apparently had a way to find a mythical dealer of souls. Or was this Dannon character David himself?

I followed quietly, unsure of what to expect but trusting Benjamin wholeheartedly. The exterior of the home was just a glimpse of what was inside. Dimly lit rooms where bleak rays of sun filtered in through dirty curtains, catching all the bits of dust that floated in the air. Strange, jagged shapes were shoved off in corners–furniture covered in sheets.

Our footsteps echoed off the empty walls and again as we ascended a grand marble staircase to the second floor. Immediately, my skin reached for the warmth of a fire burning in a large hearth to the left, the scent of rum, and some kind of roasted meat. Endless amounts of crates were stacked all around. Each bearing the insignia of various merchants and fleets. A man sat behind a massive block of a desk, flanked by two overgrown dogs, their breed completely lost to me. They looked like a mix between a German Sheppard and a Great Dane. Their thick necks were wrapped in chains that led to the desk and they sat dutifully.

"Awfully brave of you to just stroll on in unannounced," the man spoke cheekily and lit a fat cigar. He swung his feet down from the top of the desk and took a big swig of rum from a mug. "And you bring no goods with you?"

Benjamin stood stiffly, eying the man. "Dannon, I presume?"

Dannon raised his brows. "The one and only."

He stood from the worn wingback chair he sat in and I could better examine the guy. Well-dressed, better than expected for the state of the home. A leather button vest hung open over his crisp white blouse and matched the pants he wore. He was older, much older than either of us, but wore his age well with a cleanly shaven face and slicked back white hair.

"Now," he added as he leaned back against the front of his desk. "What can I do for you?" Dannon motioned to our general appearance. "I see no goods to trade, so I assume you either want to buy from me or have information to share."

"Neither," Benjamin replied gruffly. "I've come to collect something that's been held here for safekeeping."

"Oh?" Dannon raised curious brows and puffed on his cigar. But I caught the slightest flicker of his gaze as it darted to the fireplace. "Is that so?"

"Yes." Ben's hands clenched at his sides. "My brother left something here with a previous marketeer. A sword."

Dannon guffawed. "The *previous* marketeer? Dear boy, I've been running this establishment for nearly forty years. I highly doubt any brother of yours dealt with my father."

"No, not your father," Ben said. "Your grandfather. A man by the name of Branson."

Dannon's eyes flicked to the fireplace once again, and this time Ben caught it. "Branson would be my grandfather, indeed." He swallowed nervously. "But I still don't see how it's possible that your brother would have dealt with him."

Benjamin heaved a heavy and impatient sigh as he stalked over toward the fireplace. "Don't you know by now, hardly anything is impossible, Dannon." His large fingers crawled over the brickwork until he found what he was looking for and slammed the base of his fist against a loose stone. A long and narrow chamber opened up, revealing a sword. "Surely, being in this position, you've seen things." He plucked the weapon from its hiding place. "Know things."

"How did you–" Dannon whomped out his cigar in a large amber dish. "All I know of that sword is that it's cursed. My father warned me never to remove it from the hearth. Doing so would unleash unescapable darkness over the land."

Ben held the blade straight up, letting it catch the sun, and admired it with a sort of pained longing. "Well, your father wasn't wrong." His eyes moved across the room and landed on me. "This is a weapon like no other."

I squinted to examine the sword in his hand and noted how the oversized hilt was carved of bone, inlaid with sea glass, and filled with sand. Was that what we needed to find Davy Jones? Abraham's old, ornate, and strange sword? And why would Ben's brother keep it here, hidden?

"How is that going to lead us to David Jones?" I asked.

"*David Jones*?" Dannon squawked and made a move for the weapon. Ben swung the blade in the space between them, forcing the man to step back. "I-I...you cannot seriously be looking to resurrect that beast? Why unleash that on us? There wouldn't be a safe shore for miles."

Benjamin chortled. "Miles? There'd be no place on Earth you could hide from him."

"Why, then?" Dannon asked.

Benjamin swung the sword again, this time pointing its tip right at me. "Because I made a lady a promise, and this is the only way." The blade made a *schwing* sound as he flung it toward Dannon and nicked the tip of his nose. The two statue-like dogs revealed their teeth with a snarl. "Now, about those slave children outside."

Despite having the tip of a sword in his face, Dannon scowled at the mention. "What about them? They are my property to be leased out."

"Your *property*?" Benjamin bit and took a step toward the man, causing him to back up. The dogs barked. "They're children. Babies. You'll release them immediately or lose your head, good sir."

I gasped. "Ben..."

Behind his back, he shooed a hand at me. I held my breath in wait and stood off to the side.

"Call off the hounds," he ordered. Dannon

nodded and snapped once. The two dogs went rod stiff. "Now, how much to release them?"

Dannon quivered. "Well, a price is merely–"

The blade broke the surface of the skin of his cheek and Benjamin lowered his brow over his glaring stare. "How. Much."

Dannon took a few quick breaths. "They're not for sale."

Benjamin let his head lull, and he stared down at his boots with a reluctant sigh. My heart beat wildly in my chest with anticipation.

He raised his head and pursed his lips. "Wrong answer."

Before I could muster a single word, the blade sunk into Dannon's chest and I stood frozen in horror at what I was witnessing my sweet Benjamin do. I watched, mouth gaping silently as the life drained from the man's face and his body slunk to the floor.

"Ben..." the word was hardly a whisper.

He didn't look at me as he spun around and unlatched the chain that tethered the dogs. They took off down the hall and out of the house. No real loyalty to their master to be found.

"It had to be done, Dianna," he replied with a scowl. "The world will be better for it. Plus..." He raised it, and the sword in Ben's hand suddenly pulsed with life. The blood on the blade slid down toward the hilt and seeped into the dry bone. Through the windows of sea glass, I watched the idle sand swirl and move like a tornado.

"What the hell is this?" I asked.

"David Jones' sword."

I balked at his response. "What? How did you get this?"

His shoulders slumped, and he loosened a deep sigh. "Just another one of Abraham's coveted treasures. He had a knack for pissing off mythical beings."

A guffaw hiccupped in my chest. "You think?"

"This sword is made from the same bone that David's ship is made of. The sand in the hilt is earth. With this, he could harvest souls from the sea *and* the land. But without it..."

It all clicked together. "He couldn't follow you."

"Exactly," Benjamin replied. "In fact, the beast was bound to the sea and the location of the sword. So, he's been lurking beneath the surface of the ocean just outside. Unable to venture anywhere else. Pirates and sailors around the world were finally free to sail the sea without the worry of being recruited board The Flying Dutchman."

"And that's how Abraham convinced the old marketeer to keep it here," I finished for him.

We stood in stony silence. I tried not to pay attention to the body that bled out on the floor just a few feet away. I was certain if I possessed my emotions that they'd surely possess me in that moment. My mind raced with thoughts, struggled to make sense of the sudden turn of events.

"We were men when we returned to this place,"

he breathed. "Established pirates, feared even. Abraham had made a name for himself, but he wanted the ultimate prize. Control over the soul harvester that plagued our seas."

Ben stopped and thoughtfully turned the sword over in his hands. I couldn't imagine how difficult it must have been for him to return to this place, to drum up all these horrible memories.

He did it for you...

"I wish you'd told me," I said.

"You wouldn't have come," he replied with certainty. "I know you would never have let me bring you across the sea and do this if I'd told you the price. And I knew this was the only way."

"But you're going to release a monster, Ben." I took a step toward him and he stiffened. "I could have just asked the sirens."

"No," he said, and his eyes locked on mine. "I would never let you do that. Not after what I..."

He couldn't get the words out and I cupped my hand over his cheek. He relaxed into it as if he'd been holding his breath the whole time. My thumb whisked the stressed skin beneath his eyes and I wanted nothing more to take it away, his pain, his worn-out heart. The life he'd lived wasn't meant for someone who could love as he could. The darkness that lived in me sprang to life and twirled in my chest, possessing my limbs. I lowered my thumb and dragged it across his bottom lip. His hot breath poured out over and caress the skin of my hand and I parted my lips.

His hand shot up and seized my wrist, tearing my hand away from him. Without a word, he turned and stomped out of the room and I followed after I took a moment to collect myself. And for the first time since leaving Scotland, I worried for him. How much of himself was he sacrificing to return me to Henry? And here I was, throwing myself at him when I knew very well that nothing in this world would make him happier. I was dangling a carrot in front of a rabbit, knowing full well that the rabbit couldn't have it.

What kind of monster had I become?

CHAPTER ELEVEN

I ran through the empty mansion and bolted down the stairs after Benjamin, but he'd already gotten a good head start on me. He was halfway across the property and bound for the old iron gate that surrounded it.

"Wait!" I called as I speedily walked. "Benjamin!" He didn't turn, but I finally reached him and grabbed at his arm. He spun around and stared daggers down at me. "What the hell is wrong with you?"

"What's wrong with *me*?" he chided. "I'm not the one acting strange, Dianna."

"You just *killed a man*," I reminded, my chest heaving tightly.

A piff of impatient air puffed from his mouth and

he paced in place. "Dannon was no more a man than his father or grandfather before him. Scourge at best. Pearl harvesting was the best any of those children could hope for. You don't want to know what other things he leased those kids for." He took a deep breath. "I did the world a favor. Plus," he held up the sword, "I needed the blood to activate this."

"That's not the point," I argued.

"Then what is?" his voice thundered through my chest. I'd never seen him so upset.

I squared my jaw. "I worry that you're doing all this to get me home, but you still have to live in this time. *You* will have to deal with the aftermath of your actions. Unleashing a monster on the sea...a sea you'll soon have to cross when I'm gone."

His heavy leather boots scuffed in the dirt and he impatiently tossed the sword on the ground. His arms slapped helplessly at his sides. "What do you want, Dianna?"

I blinked through sudden confusion. "What–"

"*What*," he stalked toward me until his gargantuan height towered over me and I could smell the mix of leather and spice that always aired from him. "Do. You. Want."

I peered up into those brown eyes I adored so much, the innocence and desire to be good glistened in them. But behind that, a layer of pain I'd never understand. "I-I want..." What *did* I truly want? Being void of most emotion had left my will scattered. "To go home."

"You sure about that?" he challenged and closed in on me, forcing me to back up. "Because your behaviour lately tells me otherwise."

Heat rose through my body and flushed in my cheeks. "What do you mean?"

He was so close, just a breath between us, and his long brown waves trickled down, brushing the skin of my cheeks. A low moan turned over in his chest and I practically felt the vibration pulse toward me.

"You know damn well what I'm talking about." His voice was low but raspy. Deep and unnerving. "Do I need to remind you what you're fighting for? What you're trying to get home to." I had no reply, and I pursed my lips to keep from saying something I'd regret. His eyebrows rose. "Because you say the word, Dianna, and I'll stop. I'll bury that sword so deep in the earth no one will ever find it. I'll slaughter every siren in the sea. If it means...if you want to stay."

The world around us melted away into shadows as we stood and stared into one another's eyes. Neither of us willing to relent. I couldn't tell Benjamin that I didn't want to stay, couldn't dare say that some part of me didn't want him. Because that would be a lie. But to utter such words wouldn't be fair to him, my friend who constantly risked everything for me. I didn't deserve his love, not when I couldn't even reciprocate it. I'd done many things in my life that I regret, but letting

Benjamin love me was one of the worst. And now, I'd let this darkness, this...*evil*, enter my body, and it clawed at my insides for him. It played on my weakened will and blurred the line between who I was and who I was reluctantly becoming.

So, like the coward I was, I stepped away and let a breath of fresh air enter my lungs. He read my body language immediately and straightened his back as he let a deep sigh leave his body. I walked over to the sword on the ground and picked it up.

"So, what's your plan?" I asked him and tried to ignore the tremble in my voice. "You just expect to summon Davy Jones and hope he doesn't kill you on the spot?"

Benjamin stood with his back to me for a moment, his face cast to the sky. Eyes closed. When he seemed to have composed himself, he turned. "No. I plan to summon him and offer the sword as payment for his help. After all, I wasn't the one who stole it from him."

"And you don't think he'll just slaughter us both and take it?" I argued. "Why would he just help you?" He stood with his hands on his hips. I rolled my eyes and stalked over to hand him the sword. "We better get the others if we're going to march into a trap."

"It's not a trap," he defended.

I spun on my heel and began heading away from the mansion. "Life is a trap, Ben. The trick is figuring out how to escape in one piece."

***

"Aye, lassie," Finn churred as we clambered out of the boat that we'd rowed out to an empty beach. "Ye sure about his?"

Freya and Finn accompanied us on the quick trip to summon Davy Jones from the depths of his ocean prison. I'd hardly had the words out of my mouth when Finn grabbed his sword and told us to lead the way. Freya instructed the deckhands to stay behind and safeguard the ship, and to sail it home in the event that she didn't return. Her lack of faith sat heavy in my gut.

"Ask Ben," I replied. "It's his plan."

Benjamin hauled the tow rope across the sand and tied it to a tree before turning to face us and wiped his hands together. "There's no reason this shouldn't work. I'll summon David and offer the trade. As long as we stay on land and away from the shore, we'll be safe. He can't step a foot on solid earth without this sword."

Finn looked to me with a hint of concern, and I gripped the hilt of the sword that hung at my side. "But, just in case things go South, be ready."

He nodded dutifully and gripped the handle of his weapon before motioning for his sister to follow. Freya was geared up with a sword at her side and a bow across her back. Despite the tension that had grown between us, I was grateful for her help.

"Thanks," I told her as we followed Benjamin across the beach.

"Fer what?" she replied, her blazing hair blowing in the breeze.

I swallowed my pride. "For everything. For the ship, for coming with us. For being here today."

"Aye," she said with a sigh. "My brother loves ye like kin, Dianna." She peered at me from the corner of her eye. "That means yer kin to me, too. Whether I like it or nae."

A quiet chuckle rolled from me. "So, which is it?" She looked at me curiously. "Do you like it, or…not?"

Freya stared ahead as we continued to trudge through the warm sand. I couldn't quite read her expression, but I caught the slightest hint of a grin pinching at the corner of her mouth. "That's yet t'be determined."

The four of us came to a stop near the middle of a long stretch of beach. A vast stretch of land behind us. And, most importantly, no one around to get caught in the crossfire.

"Take a few steps back," Benjamin instructed, and we put about twenty feet between ourselves and the water. "Good, good," he added nervously. "Now, stay there."

We watched as he headed toward the shoreline, and I cringed when he took a knife from his pocket and dragged the blade across his palm. Even from twenty feet away, I saw the luscious crimson pool to the surface and fill his cupped hand. I held my breath while he squatted and submersed his bloody hand into the water and muttered something none of us could hear from where we stood.

I wasn't sure what to expect, what to look for, but the breath I held went cold and tight in my throat as I realized that...nothing was happening. My eyes raked over the gentle wave, scanning for any sign of movement. The sound of our heavy breathing clashed with the rushing waves and the sea fowl that circled in the distance. Benjamin walked backward and joined us in our watch.

"Maybe he can't be called," I suggested. "Maybe too much time has passed."

"No," Benjamin said with certainty and kept his unblinking stare on the water. "He's coming. I can feel it."

"How—" And I suddenly felt it, too.

The earth below trembled, and the sand started to shift under our feet. What was solid seconds before was now turning to quicksand faster than I could process it in my mind. The air became dead, and I gasped as I turned to run, but it was too late. My feet were held in place, anchored by some otherworldly force in the water that now rose above the toes of my boots.

I looked to Finn and Freya, but they were in the same situation and fought uselessly against the hold. We were like toy soldiers, bound at the feet with nowhere to run. At least Benjamin had the right mind to run back toward the beach. I craned my neck and threw him a glance over my shoulder. Benjamin's wide-eyed stare sparkled with regret and looked to me apologetically. In the near distance, the sea pulled away from us, sucking in on itself, and we had no choice but to stand there and watch as the tip of a massive vessel began to emerge from beneath the surface.

"Ladies! Brace yerselves!" Finn bellowed at me and his sister.

It seemed to never end. Just a constant length of off-white bone, carved and rounded in places where cannons and portholes lined the sides. When it finally fully emerged and slapped on top of the water like a fat whale, an enormous wave pulsed across the shore and there was nothing I could do to stop it from forcing me down under. With my feet firmly planted, I took on the full lashing of the water. Sucked it in through my mouth, my nose, my arms flailing helplessly. When my lungs burned from the salt and lack of oxygen, an arm scooped in and yanked me upward.

I gasped for air and it fought its way in through the water that I coughed up at the same time. An arm's distance away, Freya stood half soaked up to her neck. Her long red hair drenched and glued to her tall frame. She gave me a quick nod, and I mirrored it. We had no time to exchange words.

At the far end of our modest line, Benjamin's face paled, and I noted how he tucked the sword to the back of his belt. In the space between the ship and us, a figure emerged from the depths of the water. Not a man, but not a creature like anything I'd ever seen before.

Davy Jones.

Humanoid in form with two arms and legs, a head on top, but his appearance was comprised of a variety of scales. Shimmery siren flesh in some places, while the blubbery skin of a whale made up others. Tooth and bone and kelp dangled from his limbs as he stalked toward us, and we had no choice but to stand there and await his approach. When he was just a few feet away, I noticed his hollow torso, empty–save for the dirty seawater that sloshed inside–and encased in sea glass.

"Who dares summon me?" he demanded with moist lips that slapped together like drenched bits of flesh.

"You mean *resurrect* you?" Benjamin replied gruffly from the beach.

Davey's large fisheyes ogled Ben with scrutiny and a flash of recognition twinkled there. "You, boy. I've seen your soul before."

"Yes," Benjamin affirmed. "You nearly took it from me many years ago."

I threw a glance at Finn and Freya from the corner of my eye, but they just stared ahead, unblinking at the sight of this monstrosity of a being. Like a heap of discarded sea life. He was already drying in the sun, and the stench of fish wafted toward me.

"And you escaped?"

With a grin, he revealed the sword from behind his back. "Barely." Davey's eyes lit up with anger. "My brother took this from you a lifetime ago."

Davey moved swiftly between us and stopped where the brim of the sea met the sand so he could face Benjamin. "*You*! You cursed me to this eternal prison!"

Ben clucked his tongue and waved a taunting finger. "No, my brother, Abraham, did. I was merely caught in the crossfire. I wanted no part in it, no more than I do now."

"And you come to rectify the sins of your kin now, do you?" Davey chided sarcastically.

"Not exactly," Ben replied and made a show of admiring the sword in his hands. "I came to make a deal."

"A deal?" guffawed Davey. "I should drown you where you stand."

Benjamin laughed purposefully. "Where I stand is beyond your reach. And if you want this sword in one piece, I suggest you listen to what I have to offer."

Davey moved with unnerving slick sounds as he crossed his deformed fin-like arms. "I may not be able to touch you, but your friends are at my mercy." They entered a stare down for what felt like an eternity, but it was Davey who succumbed. "You have one minute, boy, before I fill their pretty bodies with seawater."

Benjamin tipped his chin toward me. "My friend is looking to get her soul back. And, since that's what you deal in, I thought you could help."

"I do not possess the girl's soul."

"We know that," Ben replied. "But surely you

could find it for her? Or, at the very least, tell us how we can retrieve it?"

He inhaled long and deep. "I'll make your deal. But the terms are that I shall look for your friend's soul, and you'll return my sword, unscathed."

"Just as you'll leave us," Ben added. "Unharmed. Now and forever."

"Fine," he snapped wetly. "Agreed."

"Agreed," Ben repeated with a terse nod.

Davy Jones whipped his head around and eyed me with sharp, impatient scrutiny before sloshing through the water to come and stand at my feet. That close, the stench of rotten fish was almost too much to bear. His googly eyes turned in their socket and two slits where a nose should be widened as he inhaled the air around me.

"You positively reek of sin," he stated with disgust, and I recoiled. "Nevertheless." He snatched my hand. "Let's see what I have to work with."

Before I could process what he was doing, Davey's fin-like hand revealed a sharpened piece of bone and he flicked it across my palm, slicing the tender skin. I winced as he squeezed my hand, drawing blood, and my stomach toiled when he brought it to his chummy lips. His tongue lapped at the blood.

After a moment of consideration, he flung my hand back at me and my arm dropped to my side. "Tell me, girl. How did you lose your soul?"

Finn, Freya, and Ben all watched me with baited

breaths, urging me. My mind scrambled for a response. "It's a bit of a long story–"

"Spare me the details," Davey snipped. "Who or what possesses your soul?"

I swallowed hard against the sudden dry tightness in my throat. "The sirens. I traded it to save my husband's life."

He made a sort of blech sound and shook his head. "There's nothing I can do for you."

"What?" I cried. "But the deal–"

"I swore to *look* for your soul," he reminded. "Not retrieve it. I've looked, it's not within my reach. And a deal with the sea Fae is not a deal I can meddle with." He sloshed back over to Ben and held out a slimy arm. "The sword, boy."

"No," Benjamin said, panic lacing his tone. "You deal in souls! It's what you do! There has to be a way!"

The grim reaper of the sea moaned with impatience. "I cannot retrieve her soul while it remains in the clutches of the sea Fae. She'll have to plead with them for its return." He grumbled something under his breath when Ben put even more space between them. "But...I can do something about that pesky curse she's holding onto." He turned and shot a stare at me. "Or should I say...holding onto *you*?"

"Curse?" I echoed.

"Yes," Davey replied with a snake-like expression, and he tipped his head to the side in mock concern. "The darkness you feel deep in your belly, the fingers that crawl around inside your chest." A gurgled chuckle turned over in him. "The whisper in your ear. You feel that, right?"

It stunned me. "It's a curse? You mean…"

"What did you think it was, girl?"

Freya and Finn exchanged a look of confusion. "What's this about a curse?" Finn asked.

I ignored him. "I thought…it was something I did."

In a flash, Davey was in my face again and I leaned back with a yelp. "No, dear. All you did was provide this lovely body for the evil to burrow in. Soul or not, it would have happened because the sirens planted it–" he poked a pointed fin at my chest. "Right here."

Finn groaned a little too loudly. "Ye mean the wretched sea beasts cursed her, even after she gave them her bloody *soul*?" He turns to me. "Why didn't ye tell me?"

I shrugged. "I didn't really know. Besides, what could you have done? You were already doing so much to help me."

"Dianna…" he replied disappointedly.

Suddenly, a thought occurred to me. Darkness, a whisper taunting me to do bad things, the emotions that made me human…gone. I motioned to Davey. "Can you tell me what kind of curse it is?"

"Not entirely," he replied. "But it's rooted deep." Davey chuckled evilly. "The sea Fae must truly despise you."

I tried to swallow, but my throat was dry as a

bone. "No, not me. My family. The whole female line of Cobhams." If I could muster a tear, my eyes would surely brim with them and I looked at Finn, who was the only one who'd truly understand the weight of my realization. He paled, eyes wide, and gave me a slow pitiful nod. "They cursed me like they did Maria. If I don't soon fix it, I'll..."

"Turn into a soulless, murderous bitch just like yer sister," Finn finished for me in a gentle, defeated tone.

I narrowed my eyes at Davey. "How do I break the curse?"

A quiet chuckle built inside of him and rose until it released in a loud, wet sound that filled the air as his back arched backward. He stuck a hand out at Benjamin. "The sword first."

Ben checked with me and I nodded. Reluctantly, he held the sword out, and the flesh of Davey's arm wrapped around the hilt, absorbing the solid shape until it fused with his body. Immediately, the sea receded, releasing the three of us, and we ran for the beach.

Davey turned to head back toward his ship, but Ben's voice cut through the air as he held me back with a protective arm. "The curse, David!"

He only stopped briefly and cast a look over his hunched shoulder. "There are but two ways. The girl can take her chances and beg the sirens to remove it."

I glanced down at the sleeves of my jacket that were stained with the sea Fae's blood. "That's...not an option," I said.

"Then the only other way is to die."

"*Die*?" we all exclaimed.

"Yes," he replied. "You must die in order for the curse to leave your body. It'll have no use for you if you're gone."

I felt the hot tension radiating from Ben's body at my side. "And how do you expect us to just let her die?"

"That's for you to figure out," Davey said without a care. "Now, I've done my part, boy." His unnerving glare narrowed at all of us. "I'll hold my end of the bargain and I trust our paths never cross again."

Benjamin glowered at him. "Not if I can help it."

And just like that, as quickly as he appeared, he was gone. Aboard his ship and we all stood wordlessly as we watched it dive back beneath the sea. No trace left behind that a giant, cursed ship of bone was ever there.

And we were no better off than before. I still had no soul, and now the darkness in me had a name. *A curse.* If I could cry, I'd surely be a heap of inconsolable human flesh on the ground. Instead, my rational mind raced through the possibilities, considered all my options.

"Aye," Freya spoke, and she looked at me with pity. "We'll find another way, Dianna. We wullnae stop until we find yer soul and get ye home."

"What do ye want to do now?" Finn asked.

I squared my shoulders and took in a deep

breath. The weight of my swift decision solid on my chest. "I want you to kill me."

CHAPTER TWELVE

"**A**hhg! I give up!" Finn bellowed impatiently as he shoved at my chest and sprung to his feet. "If Henry knew me lips were on yers he'd surely rip through time and take me head off!" He mauled a hand over his tousled beard. "If I dinnae break yer bloody ribs first!"

"It's supposed to feel like that," I told him as I sat upright and tried to hide the wince that forced from me. I could already feel the bruising taking hold where Finn's wide and clumsy hands pushed. "You'll literally be bringing me back to life."

"I cannae do it!" he replied impatiently. It was the first time I'd ever seen him so uncomfortable. Like a gentle giant trying and failing to thread a needle. "Freya did a better job. She should be the one."

Freya shifted where she sat on a hay bail with Benjamin. I wasn't sure why he stayed and watched. He'd refused to even try practicing CPR on me after I explained how it worked.

"And she just might," I told him, averting my eyes away from the other two. "I want you all to know what to do. It's a group effort." I swallowed dryly. "We're talking about my *life* here."

Finn paced frantically in the dirt and ran his fingers through his dishevelled red hair. "Ye cannae put that on me, Dianna. Helpin' ye stay alive is one thing. Bringin' ye back from the dead...I'm nae sure I can do it."

"Fine," Ben huffed and stood from where he sat. It was the first word he'd said since we began practicing. He peered down at me with a heavy sigh. "Show me."

"Are you sure?" I asked him.

"Like you said." Benjamin knelt beside me, his brown eyes glistening beneath his furrowed brow. "It's your life."

Just his mere proximity was enough to rouse the curse in the hollow of my chest. Giving an extra pulse to my heart. My skin buzzed, itching for his touch. But I stomped it down and laid back.

"Okay," I said and adjusted my shoulders. "Once I'm gone, what's the first thing you do?"

He thought for a second. "Check your...pulse?"

"Correct." I lifted my hand to put two fingers right over the spot on my throat and then my wrist, showing him where to check. "Don't start the CPR until I'm dead." His expression flickered with pain at the mention of it. "We'll have one shot, I don't want to waste it. If I'm unconscious but not dead, doing CPR will bring me back, but it won't break the curse. There needs to be *no* heartbeat. Understand?"

He just nodded reluctantly. His expression was blank as I watched him retreat behind those eyes I loved so much. What was happening inside that mind of his?

"Now, what do you do next?"

Ben's lips pursed; his palms rubbed over his bent thighs. "I...can't remember."

I made myself as flat as possible. "Check my airways, make sure nothing is blocking it. Then tip my chin upward and open my mouth wide." He listened intently. "Then push on my chest thirty times before pinching my nose and covering my mouth with yours. Then blow long and deep, twice." Ben's head bobbed as he continually nodded. "Got it?"

"I think so."

He repeated all the steps I'd told him, only pushing on my chest gently. Maybe watching Finn butcher it made him conscious of how easily he could hurt me. The bruising already forming on my chest plate throbbed with every one of his gentle pushes. But I remained still. After the thirty compressions, he paused and looked me in the eye. As if to ask permission for what he was about to do. I gave him a stern nod.

Slowly and with trembling fingers, he pinched my nose and lowered his mouth to mine. His other hand gingerly held my chin, and his fingers caressed my cheek, sending a wave of goosebumps scouring down my body. Immediately, the curse wailed inside of me, clawing at my organs, screaming through my limbs. My body went stiff while I fought to contain it, but Benjamin felt the change and when the tip of my tongue touched his, he ripped himself away.

Shame filled me like warm liquid and the curse relished in it. My eyes went wide as I sat up. "Ben, I–"

He raised his hand and shook his head. "No, don't. It's..." he seemed suddenly aware of two sets of eyes watching us from behind his back. He took a calming breath. "I think I got it."

I pressed my lips together, unable to even look at Finn and Freya as I stood and collected myself. "That's, uh, enough for today, anyway." I brushed the dust and dirt from my pants while Freya's glare burned into the side of my face. I didn't dare look at either of them, just turned toward the tavern where we were staying. "I need a drink."

***

Hours later, I paced around my room where I'd stowed myself away. A half-empty bottle of rum in hand. I wasn't fit to be around anyone, not with a wild tempestuous curse seething just under the surface of my skin, waiting for a way out. Ben seemed to be the main trigger and if I could manage to keep a healthy distance between us until I broke the curse, then maybe, just *maybe*, our friendship could survive this.

A knock at the door gave me a startle, and I hesitated.

"Dianna, it's me," Freya's voice sounded from the other side.

I unlatched the chain lock and twisted the knob, not bothering to even open the door for her. She could let herself in. But I immediately sighed in disappointment at my own self. That was petty. I opened it a crack, and she poked her lovely, freckled face inside.

"May I come in?"

I gestured toward a chair. "Please, do." I put the bottle of rum to my lips and drank heavily as she placed herself in the center of my room.

When I looked at her, she gave me a stony expression and an arched brow. "Plan to drink yerself t'death?"

I shrugged and set the bottle down with a bit too much force. "It's one way to do it." When the silence carried on too long, I let out an impatient moan and slumped into the seat she didn't take. "Come to talk me out of my plan?"

Freya crossed her arms over the faded blue linen dress she wore. "Quite the opposite, actually. I cannae wait fer ye to break this bloody curse."

"Is that so?" I had no idea why I was being so cold

with her. Freya and I started off as friends when we first arrived in Scotland. But the journey across the Atlantic, the tension we tossed back and forth over Benjamin...we were different people now. "Hoping to get rid of me so soon?"

Freya tilted her head to the side. "Nae, I just want ye to stop toying with Benjamin's heart."

I averted my gaze. "Ben's a big boy."

"Aye," she replied tiredly. "A man. A man who's so blindly in love with ye it's killin' him." Anger rose in my gut and my knee bobbed up and down impatiently. "But he could love me. In time. If...if ye let him."

I guffaw practically choked me. "*Let* him?"

"Ye have t'let him go, Dianna," she reasoned calmly. "Tell him there's no chance, it'll never happen. He can never have ye and he should move on."

"I don't need to do that," I seethed through clenched teeth. "Ben knows where I stand, where *we* stand as friends. He knows Henry is my soulmate."

She stood over me from a few feet away and chewed at the inside of her lip. "Aye, but now he thinks yer goin' t'give up tryin' to get back to yer *soulmate*." My eyes narrowed at her accusatory tone. "He thinks...there's a chance fer him now."

"Get out," I said in a clipped tone and glowered up at her from my chair.

She waited a beat then turned on her heel and reached for the door. I swiped the rum from the table and tossed my head back as I put it to my lips and drank until I heard the latch fall into place and I was alone again.

Alone and empty of everything except the liquor that burned in my belly. With nothing but time and the expanse of my room before me, I wandered about. Noting the hand-carved details of the woodwork. The log embedded in the wall above the fireplace used to display half-burned candlesticks and brass trinkets like a clock and empty picture frames. The uneven and burnt wood floor, worn and shiny in places where years of past guests occupied the room. The window was open and blew a cool early evening breeze inside, making the thin cream-colored draperies billow softly. It had everything required to be a room, but it wasn't a home. I suddenly and oddly felt akin to it. A body, a person. Yet, empty inside.

With a disgruntled moan, I threw myself onto the bed and let all my tired, achy muscles relax. My finger hooked through the handle on the bottle of rum and it dangled off the side as I stared up at the bottom of the canopy that covered the four-poster bed. Freya's words moved to the forefront of my mind and I rolled them over and over. Considered every syllable. But I kept circling back to the same conclusion.

She was right.

And I wondered then, what a life with Ben would be like. He was handsome and loyal. Kind and strong. I'd once told him that in another time they surely would have been together. And here I was...stranded in another time, lost with no way back to the man I truly loved. Even as I considered it, the thoughts felt wrong in my mind.

I knew it was the curse that evoked that behaviour from me. But part of me couldn't help but wonder if I could have fought harder to stomp it down. When it wanted to wake up, I practically stepped aside and let it. Every time. Guilt couldn't tug at my emotions, but it still rattled in my rational mind. Rum swirled in my veins, hot and sweet, and I set the jug on the floor before rolling over to conjure up memories of Henry to fend off thoughts of anything else.

First, I pulled him into my mind's eye. Shaped him and highlighted all the features of his existence. Every scar, every blade of golden hair, the way the light could never penetrate those black eyes as they touched my soul.

My soul...

My eyelids became heavy with the threat of sleep, but I fought it. I couldn't face a nightmare. Not after the nightmare I'd lived all day. I grappled to hold on to the memories of Henry. My sweet pirate king. I let my eyes close, but only to better envision his hands on my body, caressing every sensitive spot as they held me tenderly. I brought my fingertips to my lips as I imagined his mouth there, kissing me and stealing the breath right from my lungs. Desire and yearning filled me, pushing back the confusion I felt emanating from the curse that lived there. *This is what you wanted, isn't it?* I asked it silently. *This is what you feed on.*

Reality slowly melted away as I sunk into a dream. Completely helplessly against the throes of sleep. But I was pleasantly surprised to find no nightmare in sight. No darkness filling the corners of that empty room. Instead, I laid on a sunny beach while hot rays soaked into my skin. Above me, a figure moved and blocked the sun, his hair dangling around his shadowed face and tickling my skin.

Henry...

A rush of warm goosebumps coated my body at the touch of his hand on my inner thigh beneath the light sundress I wore. He spread my legs and lowered himself, nestling comfortably and placing my slender, trembling limbs around his torso. One hand held my face, rubbed my cheek, and traced the lines of my open and waiting mouth as a fiery breath poured from it.

His other hand slipped between us where our centers met, and my back arched with the force of a gasp that buckled my entire body. Henry's fingers moved like waves, leading us both into a sensual rhythm. His mouth was on mine, preventing any cries of pleasure, and I raked my fingers through his long hair.

Impossibly long...

Every time my thoughts strayed, the confines of the dream pulled me back into the moment and I let myself become consumed by the man who had me caged to the sand with his body.

An unfamiliar shape...

It was hard to turn my head through the fog that filled it, and Henry's powerful grip on my jaw firmed, holding me there and forcing me to look at his shadowed face while his mouth continued to dance against mine. While somewhere in the back of my mind shouted distantly for me to wake up, I couldn't leave him. I couldn't leave behind this feeling of...being alive. My desire for him ran hot and only intensified with every encompassing kiss until I could hardly stand it.

I stole a breath and whispered through heavy panting, "I want you."

His hand that remained between my legs tore down my undergarments and as he thrust himself inside of me, the sun moved to reveal his face. Only...it wasn't him.

"Ben!" I cried as our bodies moved in unison against the sand.

Every wave of his hips sent me reeling with bliss, and I threw my head back as he buried himself deep inside. Moans of both pleasure and guilt poured from me and filled the hot air around us. His quickened breaths and deep moans of carnality blanketed me, and I let myself become consumed by him until I felt the climax of release building up inside. Every thrust became harder and quickened to the point of breaking, and the dream shattered around me like glass as we came together.

I woke with a startle and bolted upright, my

hands instantly grappling at my chest, desperate to hold on to reality for fear of dipping back into the dream. How could my mind conjure such a thing? I trembled all over, despite the fact that I was covered in sweat.

Henry...I buried my face in my hands and, for the first time in months, my eyes filled with tears. Who was this person I was becoming? What kind of wife, partner, soulmate was I to let myself fall victim to my own inexcusable desires? The tears gave way to a dam of locked-up emotions and cleared the way for a second of rational thinking. That wasn't *my* desire. Making love to Benjamin was never something I would ever dream up. Which meant...

It wasn't a dream. It *was* a nightmare, after all. Visions and senses that the curse drummed up in my head. Blatantly showing me what it wanted, and how far it was willing to go to get it. And, in that moment, I realized just what kind of curse the sirens planted inside of me. A living darkness that would never stop until it shaved away my will, cut down my ability to feel until I was an empty vessel for it to animate. It wanted me to destroy myself, so there was nothing left to go back to.

Clever girl.
Foolish girl.
She knows.
She's ours now. There is no escape.

The whispers of the sea Fae overlapped with each word and rang in my ears, causing my head to spin as a cold inky sensation spilled from my heart and reached out through my limbs, filling every pore. Every finger. Every crack of my being. I had no choice but to let it consume me, and my body went stiff as it slammed back onto the bed. Darkness touched the edges of my vision, slowly pressing in until I couldn't see anything, and I plunged into an abyss.

CHAPTER THIRTEEN

BENJAMIN

Just as my thoughts of the day, my dreams at night were of her. Of Dianna. Try as I might, I couldn't stop it. Couldn't stop the images and the desires that floated around freely in my mind. I rolled over in the darkness of my quarters in the brothel after a sound in the hallway roused me from sleep. I didn't open my eyes for fear I wouldn't be able to sink back into the bliss of a dream, one where she and I were together. The only place we'd ever be together like that.

But another sound, the creaking of the floor near the foot of my bed, pulled my drowsy consciousness to the surface, and I opened my eyes to see what was there. In the pitch black of the room, I saw nothing. But I knew, could sense, something was there. I waited and stared at the furs draped over the foot of the bed, at the small patch of white moonlight that cut across it from a sliver in the draperies. A lump moved under the blankets, heading for my feet, and I tensed when a delicate hand brushed the naked skin of my legs.

Was this a dream?

I reached under and pulled back the bedding to reveal a face clouded in shadow, but I'd know the shape of her anywhere and my heart banged in my chest.

"Dianna?" I whispered, not believing my eyes.

Her voice moaned in the darkness as she crawled up my body and only when the warm skin of hers touched my bare chest did I realize she was naked. I gripped her arms and pushed her off as I sat upright.

"*Christ*, Dianna." My voice hitched. Her hands continued to paw at me, her loose black curls tickling my warm skin. "What are you doing?"

"I want you." Her voice was low and in my ear. The same lips I stared at from afar each day. Under the sheets, her legs parted, and she shifted to straddle me. "And I know you want me."

"Woah!" My mind and body slammed together with separate wants, and I gripped her hips to slip out from beneath her. But she squeezed me like a vice. "Jesus..."

"Benjamin," her oddly musical voice purred in the night and her presence enamoured me in place. I was afraid to touch her, for fear of crossing a line she so clearly wanted to make disappear. *Was she sleepwalking?* A perfect finger trailed down my chest. "Don't you want me?"

I brought my hands to her neck and my giant mitts engulfed the whole area; her face relaxed into the touch. Her mouth covered my thumb, sending almost painful goosebumps up my spine. "Of *course*, I want you," I told her and gritted my teeth against the urge to take her right there. "But…Henry."

She shook her head and shifted to secure the grip her legs had around my waist as we sat up together. "Is in another time, in a place I'll never go back to."

My heart thundered at her words and my throat tightened. "You're giving up?"

"Not giving up," she cooed sensually and rolled her hips, driving a taut moan from me. "Accepting what is. The sirens will never give me back my soul, no matter how much I beg, no matter what I offer in trade. This is my home now; this is my life." Her face dipped to my ear and I shuddered at the drag of her teeth across my lobe. "And I want it to be with you."

I'd dreamed of those words spilling from her lips. For years. Imagined a thousand scenarios where Dianna would finally be mine, in a reality where I didn't have to live with the guilt of taking her away from the man she loved. Because I never wanted to do that, to *take her*. It wouldn't be right. I wanted *her* to take *me*. I wanted *her* to *want me*. But I'd long accepted that it would never be more than hopes and dreams.

Yet…here she was. Giving herself to me.

I sat up further but let her remain in my lap, terrified that if I moved her, she'd disappear with the lucid dream I was certain I was having. I held that sweet face in my hands, put her forehead to mine, and breathed. In and out. Focused on what I knew to be real. I was real, the room, the bedding, the cool night breeze that floated in through the open window.

And she was real. And naked. And…in my bed.

"Dianna," I whispered against her face. Tears threatened to come, but I bit them back. "Are you certain…this is what you want?"

She nodded in my hands and I brushed my thumb across her bottom lip, readying her mouth to take. Slowly, I leaned in, savouring every second of the moment that I'd dreamed of for years. I inhaled the scent of her; a mix of soap and ocean air laced with…*rum*? The heat that pulsed from her naked skin soaked into me and burrowed in the sheets that pooled around us. I hauled her closer, tightening the connection our bodies made, and hovered my mouth over hers.

But it didn't feel right.

I hesitated. "Maybe we should wait–"

"*Wait for when?*" her voice cut through the room like shattered glass.

"For when your breath doesn't reek of rum," I told her as I swam out of the fog of bliss.

I tried to slide back a bit, to get a look at Dianna's face that remained in the shadows. I noted her breathing then, how it was different. Not like the soothing rhythmic hum I'd come to know better than my own. I grabbed her arms and fought to move her into the sliver of moonlight that cut across the bed. Her eyes, completely black to the rims, flashed with anger and an unnerving sound screeched in her throat like iron against glass.

She fled from the bed in a flash and I bolted for the door before she could escape, slammed it shut, and hatched the lock. I pressed my back up against the cool wood as I scanned the room. But it was so dark. I could hear her scuttling around, but it was too damn hard to see.

Frantically, I reached for the console next to the door to swipe a candle and some matches. Some fell and trickled to the floor as I blindly lit the wick, refusing to take my eyes off any movement I found in the room's darkness. When the flame came to life, I held it out in search of her.

The room fell silent. Only the quick in and out of my own ragged breathing touched my ears and I waited. Frozen in place.

"Dianna?" I said cautiously and dared move away from the door. My heavy foot caused the floor to creak and, as fast as lightning, she appeared from behind the canopied bed in a flicker. As if manifesting from thin air. My eyes bulged at the sight of her and I nearly dropped the candle. "Christ…"

I wished her bared form were shocking enough, but it was the black veins that crawled over her entire body like spilled ink. Moving, alive, and pulsing like a heartbeat. Her blackened eyes glared at me from beneath her lowered brow.

"Dianna is gone." The voice had changed again, this time its glassy tone scratched at my ears and I winced. "Now she's all ours." A sneer spread across her lips. "All *yours*, Benjamin Cook."

Rage built in my chest. "Bloody sirens." She only cackled eerily under her breath. "Dianna, I know you're still in there. Somewhere. Follow the sound of my voice. Come back to me."

"You waste your energy," she replied coldly. "There's only one way to save her now." Faster than I could process, she flickered and appeared right in front of me, her breath on my face as she grinned wildly. A pointed finger jabbed deep into my stomach, threatening to break the skin, and I stifled a cry of pain. "And you don't have the *guts* to do it."

Calmly, as if to not alert the beast of the thoughts rolling over in my mind, I set the candlestick down on the console and leaned my face in, touching my nose to hers. When I had an arm secured around her back, I said, "You have *no* idea how far I'd go for her."

I threw my weight onto Dianna's body and pinned her to the ground as the beast inside wailed to be released. Arms and legs flailed under me, but I was far too large and far too heavy for her to even nudge. Another wail poured from her mouth and I cupped my hand over it and her nose. Her body—*it was just a body, just a body, just a body*—convulsed against the floor and I stretched out to cover as much of her as I could while I choked every last scrap of air from her lungs. It felt like an eternity and I had to bury my face in the crook of her shoulder and neck because I was too cowardly to face her when the life inevitably left her eyes.

The siren's curse was strong, embedded deep because any normal human being would have suffocated minutes ago. The fingers I used to cover her mouth and pinch her nose went numb, and I couldn't stop the tears from coming. They streamed down my face, hot and searing and never-ending as I took the life of the woman I loved.

Finally, her body deflated, and she slowly relaxed in my arms. The convulsing subsided until there was nothing but stillness in us both. I couldn't pull my hand away from her face; I was frozen, petrified, held prisoner by disbelief and guilt. Tears still streamed from my eyes, though, and pooled in her hair.

"I'm sorry!" I cried into the clammy skin of her neck and tensed with the crushing guilt. "I-I'm...*sorry*..."

When I drummed up the courage to pull away and look at her slackened face, relief flooded me when I saw that the black veins were gone, followed immediately by an uncontrollable tremble that rocked through me. She was gone. Dianna was dead. I'd...killed her. I still couldn't stop the tears, but I managed to tug a rogue sheet from the bed and cover her exposed body, leaving her head uncovered.

I knelt on the floor as my shaking hands hovered over the body, unsure where to start. I closed my eyes to focus. Called the recent memories of the afternoon when Dianna had showed me exactly what to do. When I'd moved over the steps a few times in my mind, made sure I had it right, I opened my eyes and began.

Check the pulse. Check the airway. Tip the head back. Push thirty times on the chest. Pinch nose and cover mouth with mine. Blow twice. Repeat.

After the fourth round, I worried, and panic quickened my movements. My chest compressions became harder, rougher, desperate. Still...nothing. She was a corpse on the floor, and I was the fool trying to breathe life back into a body that had been so horribly wrecked by magic.

I wouldn't stop. Someone would have to come in the early hours of the morning to bust down the door and pry my hands away from her. Even then, I wasn't sure I'd let them. "I won't give up," I spoke through laboured breaths. "I. Won't." I blew twice, forcing my own air as far into her lungs as I could. "Come on, Dianna!" I urged and pushed frantically at her fragile chest. "Come on! *Come back to me, God damn it!*"

Suddenly, she came gasping back to life with a

sharp, haunting inhale and flew upward into a sitting position. I scrambled back on my ass, stunned that I'd actually done it. The sheet fell loose, and I quickly pulled it up to cover her bare breasts, my fingers trembling, my heart in my throat. In the dim candlelight, her soft brown eyes appeared empty, but she blinked a few times and I watched as the world came back to her.

"B-Ben..." She stared at me, confused, and noted the sheet I held against her. Her cheeks flushed with color as she yanked it away from my grasp. "What the hell is going on!"

I couldn't form words, and tears still dripped down over my face. Shock possessed me. "I...they...I had no choice." Every letter crumbled like dust on my tongue. "You were...the sirens. The curse. I—I had to do it."

She shivered and took stock of herself, winced when she tried to move. Then her eyes flashed to mine and held my stare. "You broke the curse?"

Salty wetness filled the crease of my pursed lips, and I nodded. She spread a hand over her chest, slid it upward, and grasped her neck as she stared distantly into the space over my shoulder. I was falling apart from the relief that collided with guilt in my heart, but I noticed how Dianna began to tremble even more. Her emotions. I'd suspected that the curse had stifled them, and they must have been coming back to her tenfold.

And it was in that moment that I realized the stark difference between this Dianna and the one

I'd been travelling with the last few months. Like comparing the sun to a cloud. Her expression wavered through them all. Shock, sadness, anger, happiness. Every emotion filled her, finding a home, and she bent over the floor as if she were about to heave. But only pained cries leaked from her mouth. Ugly sobs and sharp breaths.

Hesitantly, I placed a comforting hand on her back. "It's okay, I'm here. I'm not leaving you to go through this alone. I'm not going anywhere."

Through the empty retching, she turned her head to face me. "That's the problem, Ben." Another sound wretched from her and I felt the tension beneath my hand. "And neither am I." She gave up and fell into a crumble on the floor. "I'm never going to get home. I'm stuck here. And now...I have to live with that pain."

I recoiled and slunk up against the foot of the bed. "Are you...upset with me?" When she didn't reply I grew angry, defensive. "Christ, Dianna, you were *gone*! The curse had taken you completely! What would you have me do?"

She slowly turned her pitiful gaze on me, tears welled in her swollen eyes. "Let me die?"

Everything be damned, I scooped her into my arms and held her as tight as I could without crushing her fragile, shattered body. "I could never do that." The words were a whisper through the tears that tickled in my throat.

She felt tense in my grasp, almost defensive, but soon softened and relaxed against my chest. After a while, when her slender arms wrapped around my torso and her tear-slicked face cuddled my chest, my heart settled knowing she'd be alright. Eventually.

CHAPTER FOURTEEN

DIANNA

The weight of human emotion was heavier than anything I could ever imagine. Being without it for so long, having adjusted to the blissful emptiness, and then suddenly having the wide range of feeling slam back into my body...it was unbearable.

After Benjamin broke the curse and my humanity switched back on, I spent two days in bed with the door locked. The madam of the brothel came to check on me a dozen times, and I knew it was just my friends showing concern but giving me space. I needed time to readjust to this...body. This life. This...existence without Henry and the kids.

On the third morning of my isolation, hunger pangs rustled me from a comfortable sleep and the sun burned my eyes. I rolled over and covered my head with the blankets, but the smell beneath them was almost too much to bear. I desperately needed a bath. And some food. My time to wallow and hide was over.

I removed the blankets just as a knock came at the door and I wasn't surprised to find the madam there with a tray of food. She'd always come to ask, but never actually brought any with her.

"How did you know—"

She shrugged and swooped in past me to set the tray of eggs and tea down on the little table by the door. "It's been days," she said. "Feed that body of yours."

She turned to leave, and I reached out to touch her arm. "Thank you," I said as she examined my tired face. "I...I don't even know your name."

She smiled and I saw the beauty she once possessed in her younger years, beneath the overly tanned skin and layers of chalky makeup. "You may call me Madam Lorretta."

My stomach growled at the scent of warm food that wafted up to my nose. "Madam Lorretta, may I trouble you for a bath?"

"Of course," she said with a grin. "I'll have one prepared for you in the bathing room." She pointed at the food. "Eat."

I chuckled, a real weighty sound that felt almost unfamiliar to me, and gave her a nod as I closed the door. After I filled my empty belly and washed away the sins that plagued me, I got dressed and headed out for some air. I had no idea where my friends were, but I was grateful they were off busy somewhere. I wasn't ready to face them, wasn't ready to deal with the way I'd treated Freya, or how I'd thrown myself at Ben. The memories of that horrific night were clouded, choppy, as if I remembered them through someone else's eyes, but they were there, nonetheless. Forever etched into my mind.

I found myself trailing along one of the many beaches that surrounded the island where we stayed. I took my boots off and let my toes dig into the sand with every step, desperate to feel anchored to the world after being disconnected for so long. I realized then that I had no idea where we really were. The Caribbean, yes, but I knew it comprised dozens of islands. Cuba? Barbados?

I guess it didn't matter.

We'd be setting sail for Scotland soon and would brave the sea once more. I wasn't sure I had it in me to traverse the waters that seemed to hate me so much. But I had no choice. I couldn't stay here. Maybe I could convince Finn to take the other route, the longer one that hugged the Eastern Coast of North America, and have him drop me off in Newfoundland. I'd still be alone but at least it was the closest thing I had to home. And, without a soul to mark the expiration of my life, I'd one day catch up to them. I'd see their faces again, and that was all I needed to keep me holding on.

I wasn't sure the reason for my wandering until now, when the truth of it suddenly dawned on me. I was coming to say goodbye. For now. Goodbye to the life I once had, to Henry, to my two beautiful children–they were cared for and loved. They had each other. I had to hold on to that. I'd rather die alone in the past, knowing that my family was safe than to make another deal with a siren. I'd had enough of the treacherous sea Fae for one lifetime.

I tossed my boots aside and plopped down in the sand. I hugged my knees tight to my chest as I stared out over the calm afternoon water. The sun sparkled on the gentle waves like flecks of gold, and I inhaled the heady salt air. As much as I despised the sea for what's it's done to me...I couldn't truly hate it in the end. It had always been a part of me; born and bred by its side, its scent infused in my blood.

I was a Newfoundlander, after all.

The walk had done me some good. Cleared my mind and set my thoughts on the right track. I could do this. I could say goodbye and make my peace until I reunited with the ones I loved a few hundred years from now. I had my humanity back, my emotions, friends who cared about me.

I picked up a rock and chucked it hard and far into the water. "You've taken from me for the last time," I told it, and, as ridiculous as I must have looked, I knew it could hear me. The sea. A timeless beast. "I'm done. I won't let you win; the Cobham curse ends here. With me."

I stood and brushed the sand from my pants before grabbing my boots. But just as I was about to turn and head back over the grassy mounds that led to the port, I noticed the edge of the water suddenly and drastically recede. I watched as the water sucked back, revealing wet and glistening rocks, and I glanced around in confusion.

"What the—"

Faster than my mind could register, the water rushed back to the shore in a tremendous wave and crashed down around me. Soaking my clothes and drenching my entire body. Anger bubbled in my gut and I wiped the water from my face with a gasp.

"For an ancient being, you're sure childish—"

There was a figure on the beach that wasn't there before. A giant lump of black leather huddled in a limp fetal position. My heart froze in my chest and I stared at it unblinkingly. To anyone else, it would have appeared to be a random body. But not to me. I'd recognize the shape of him anywhere, no matter how many centuries would pass between us. And the sea knew that.

I stumbled in the sand as I rushed to his side and turned him over with trembling hands. Disbelief pounding at my chest. But it was him, he was right there.

"Henry!"

Excitement possessed me as I took in every detail of his beautiful face, and it took me a moment to realize he was unconscious. I flew into panic mode, hauled his heavy body over fully on his back, and began CPR. Thankfully, it only took a few tries to beat the life back into him. With a gurgled gasp, his eyes flew open, and he rolled over to spew seawater from his lungs.

I rocked back and sat on my heels, practically bursting with joy. When he was done, he turned to face me with a disoriented look, but I flung myself at him, wrapped my arms so tight. And he did the same. Those long, muscled arms took me in an embrace so hard I could barely breathe. But I didn't care.

"What are you doing here?" I managed to ask, refusing to loosen my hold. After the night I'd had—heck...the few months, even—I needed this, needed *him*. But paranoia stirred in my gut. The sea gifted him to me.

Henry moved in my arms, put his face to mine, and kissed me. Long and hard and painful and blissful. As if years, not months, had passed since he'd done so. I trembled on the sand, overcome with joy and worry. I shifted my hands, only to hold his face tighter as if starved of him. His mouth moved against mine.

"I once promised I'd part the seas to find you," he replied. The sound of his raspy tone roused every new emotion in my body, and I kissed him again. He clumsily smoothed the wet hair away from my face. "Why are you crying? Are you hurt?"

I hadn't even realized I was crying. "No," I told him with a giddy laugh. "Everything is perfect now that you're here." My eyes locked on his. "Where are the kids?"

Henry's returning smile was calm and comforting.

"They're safe with your mother."

I shook my head. "How did you get here?" He didn't immediately answer, just searched my eyes, and I knew. He'd made some sort of bargain. My lips quivered, my head gently shook. "No..."

Henry took in a deep breath. "I made no trades, no deals. I combed through your office, scoured the internet–don't even," he said quickly at my look of surprise. Henry using the internet. It was one of the many modern wonders he'd dismissed so boldly. "I searched for a dealer in rare pearls."

"Did you find one?"

He shook his head, and I noted how he seemed to hide something behind those eyes. No, not hide, but...hesitated.

"Then...how?"

He slicked a hand through his soaked blond hair, smoothing it back over his head to reveal more of the face I loved and missed so much. But he was biding time.

"Henry." I laid the word down with finality.

"Audrey's sleepwalking is getting worse," he said. My limbs immediately ran cold. "After I returned home one night, late, I think...long after midnight, I found her on the front porch in her pyjamas. Soaked to the waist, barefoot. She was still asleep. So, I brought her up to bed and when I tucked her in, I saw it." He stopped to swallow nervously and reached into his pocket. "Two pearls tied with braided seaweed."

I glanced down at the single pearl he held

between his fingers, and the air squeezed from my lungs as I slipped from his embrace and plopped back on the sand.

"I used one to get here," he continued and tucked the pearl away again. "The other is to take you home."

"I-I still don't have my soul," I told him. But my mind was elsewhere. "Those god damn sirens. I wish…" I let the rest of the words die on my lips because I knew I shouldn't say it. A *wish*, but also what was about to come after it. I'd slaughtered one just days ago. The blood, while out of sight, still not out of mind, and I wondered if I'd always feel it on my hands. Even so, knowing they still meddled with my family, my children, I wanted to lay waste to the lot of them. "Is she alright?"

He nodded. "As far as I can tell. There seemed to have been no conditions attached to the gift." I guffawed at the word. *Gift*. No such thing came from the sea beasts. "But that's something we'll deal with later." He reached over and took my face in his hands and my body reacted in kind, melted at his healing touch. "For now, let's get your soul back."

"Easier said than done."

He inhaled deeply through his nose. "We'll find a way." He put his forehead to mine and part of me settled, knowing he was right. I trusted he'd find a way. He always did. *We* always did. Together.

"Wait," I said. "Where do the kids think you are?"

He laughed. "They think I'm in St. John's."

"You're a little far from St. John's."

He leaned back and took stock of his surroundings for the first time. His forehead wrinkled, and he shook his head. "Where...this isn't Scotland."

My exhausted legs protested as I pushed to my feet. I held a hand down for him to take, suddenly eager to get him off the beach for fear the sea would take him from me in some cosmic joke. "Come on," I said and helped him to his feet. "I've got a lot to tell you."

CHAPTER FIFTEEN

We took our time heading back to the village near the port. I wanted to savour every second I could. I told him all about the weeks that followed his untimely departure to the future. Lottie's disassociation, her heartbreak, Gus' funeral, our trip South, and the stopover in Portugal. About finding Davy Jones and how the effort was wasted. I skirted around details about the old woman who saw the devil in me and the siren's heart I'd pierced with Maria's dagger. For some reason, I couldn't seem to form the right words to explain. And, truthfully, I didn't want him to stop looking at me like he did. With love and admiration. We reached the brothel before I got to the more recent events. The night before, in particular. But I would tell him. When the time was right.

I hauled open the heavy wooden door and the stench of heavy perfume and body odour met my nose. Under it, a hint of food cooking. Some kind of sausage and eggs, by the look of a few plates that sat abandoned on tables.

I searched for familiar faces, but a loud and hasty stomping caught my attention and stepped out of the way just as Finn collided with Henry. My husband was a large a tall man, but Finn's gargantuan size devoured him. He lifted Henry in a crushing hug and bounced him in his arms.

"What the devil are ye doin' here, ye bloody idiot!" His words delivered on a stream of laughter and he set Henry down clumsily.

"What can I say, old friend?" Henry replied lightly. "Just couldn't stay away."

Finn slapped his arm with a bit too much force. "Aye, well, 'tis good t'see ye." He sighed gruffly, and he flashed me a look before giving Henry a pursed smile. He knew why Henry was there.

Behind Finn, Freya and Benjamin approached and exchanged pleasant greetings with Henry. But Ben was quiet and, as he stepped aside, his gaze met mine and the pain pooling in his eyes was like a knife in my heart. We still hadn't had the chance to talk about what had happened the night before. Not properly, not with me in my right mind. A deep, groveling apology lay stacked on my chest along with a massive thank you for saving me from myself. But it'd have to wait.

"You'll have to excuse me," Henry spoke to everyone and took my hand. "The…travel was daunting, and I'd like to be alone with my wife for a while." He smiled. "I'd like to convene later, though, to eat and catch up. Discuss our options."

"Of course," Finn replied and cocked his head to the others to follow him outside. He patted Henry's back. "We'll see ye later, then."

I nodded and smiled to Finn and Freya, but Ben was already gone. He'd slipped out unnoticed and my heart sank. I breathed in deeply, long and calming. Willing the guilt to push to the bottom of my gut where I'd deal with it later.

I wrapped both arms around one of Henry's and leaned against him with a tired sigh. "Come on," I told him and tugged gently. "I'll show you my room."

The second the door latched, two hands grabbed me from behind and Henry swooped me into his arms where he cradled me. His mouth immediately found mine. I wove my fingers together at the back of his head and crushed our warm lips together. He pulled away to loosen a deep moan and his whole body hummed against my skin.

"I've missed you," he whispered in a raspy purr. "*God*, I've missed you more than I can put into words."

He carried me over to the bed and laid us down together. But I put my hands on his chest before he could go any further. It wouldn't be fair, not to him, to me, to Ben, if I didn't tell him first.

"Henry," I said. "There's...there's something I need to tell you."

He read my body language and sat upright with caution. "Are you alright?"

My mind raced for a place to start. "It's still all so *fresh*," I told him as tears rimmed my eyes. "I'm sorry." He swiped the edge of a finger under my eye to catch a rogue tear, and my hands fidgeted nervously between us. "The day the Keepers told me the bad news, that...they couldn't retrieve my soul, I...a part of me sort of...died."

His forehead wrinkled as his expression turned hard. "What do you mean?"

"My emotions," I fought to explain. "They—I'd switched the off somehow. But what I didn't know, what none of us knew, was that when the sirens took my soul they left behind a curse."

"What?" Anger pulsed from him.

"But it didn't or...*couldn't* take hold until it had room," I continued. "Until I pushed my human emotions aside. Then, slowly, it grew. It festered inside of me and I had no idea until—"

My mind went blank. I had no idea how to properly explain it.

My chin dropped to my chest and Henry's face dipped to look at me with nothing but love and concern. "Until what, Dianna?" His finger gently urged my chin back up so I could look at him. "You can tell me anything."

Tears spilled over then. "I know." I kissed him. Once and gingerly before I continued to explain.

"Eventually, the curse grew powerful enough that it took over." His black eyes widened, but he let me go on. "It animated my body and wanted to use it for...God, this is so hard."

"Just tell me," he urged calmly. "Whatever it is, it's alright. Clearly, you've remedied it."

"Ben saved me," I blurted out. "After I–after the curse used my body to try and...*seduce him*." I cringed at the last two words, how they struggled to leave my throat, and waited for the angry blow of Henry's temper. I cinched my eyes in preparation. But, when silence hovered, I opened my eyes to find only a look of concern.

"Did you..." His gaze left me and focused on the blanket beneath us.

My heart squeezed. "Oh, no, nothing! Henry," I waited for him to look at me again. "*Nothing* happened. Benjamin stopped it. And then he...broke the curse before it could go any further." I didn't have the heart to tell him how. Maybe I was a coward, or maybe I valued Ben's life too much. Because if Henry discovered Ben had killed me less than twenty-four hours ago, even if it were to *save* me, I didn't want to know what he'd do.

Too much time passed without a reply from him, and panic ceased in my chest.

"Are you mad?"

"*Mad*?" he blurted. "Christ, Dianna, I'm not a complete monster. How could I be mad about something you had no control over?" The length of his throat moved with a slow swallow.

"Unless...there's something else. Unless being with Benjamin is what you truly desire. Even then, I wouldn't–"

"Never!" I exclaimed. "No, never. Henry, Benjamin is one of my best friends. Yes, I'm inexplicably linked to him by some force of the sea, some residual unknown magic we'd tapped into when I released him from The Black Soul." I stopped to take a breath and slow my words. "But friends are all we'll ever be." I shifted closer so our bodies pressed together on the bed. "You're the only one who possesses my heart. I can't believe I even have to say that after all these years. I'm yours, Mr. White. Always."

A devilish grin spread across his beautiful face and he covered me with his body, his presence. "Then allow me to take what is mine." His voice was like the ocean at night; deep, dark, rough. But underneath, soothing. Cool and calming. "Do you have any idea how badly I've wanted to touch you?" His breath caressed my ear as his fingers slipped inside my pants. "How long I've waited to be inside you?"

My head swam with him. His scent, his touch. I soaked it up as if I'd been starving of him. A deep moan pressed from my lungs and I gasped for air before letting him take my mouth and I shuddered all over. With one expert hand, Henry ripped down my pants and I hastily kicked them off, never breaking the heated kiss we shared. His warm tongue danced with mine and I grasped desperately at his back, wanting him closer. Wanting him inside of me. Every inch of me screamed for it. And when Henry slid between my legs, I threw my head back and let the bliss take me away.

***

A strange ruffling sound stirred me from sleep. My body ached, but in a good way, in a way that I never knew I missed. Henry's scent and touch were all over me, soaked into my skin, and I tucked the sheets up around my face in an attempt to contain it for as long as I could.

The sound of a boot touching the floor made my eyes fly open, and I rolled over to find Henry perched on the edge of my bed. He was fully dressed.

"Where are you going?" I asked him in a groggy morning voice. My fingers got stuck in my knotted hair.

He turned and stretched an arm over my torso to lean in and kiss me. "Morning, my queen."

I softly scratched the blonde stubble on his face. "Your queen orders you to stay in bed."

A quick laugh puffed from his throat, but I noticed how he could hardly meet my eyes. Something sprang to life in my chest, alerting me to panic. I pinched his chin between my fingers and forced him to look at me.

"*Where* are you going, Henry?"

His reply was to pull and tuck the sheets up around me. Then he stood, his long black trench coat settling around his knees.

"Henry!"

"You know where I'm going." His voice was calm, reserved, weighed down with purpose.

I bolted upright, studying his face. "No, I–" It all suddenly clicked into place. Maybe because it was painfully obvious, or maybe because I knew my husband's tortured mind better than my own. I flung the blankets off my naked body and scrambled into my grey slacks. I grabbed my shirt before slamming myself up against the door to barricade it. Henry just sighed in annoyance. "You're not going anywhere."

His brows rose challengingly. "So, what, you're just going to keep me a prisoner in this room?" His shoulders slumped tiredly. "Move out of the way, Dianna."

I shoved my arms through the sleeves of the shirt. "No, I can't let you go to them. I can't–"

"Dianna!"

I hadn't seen that dark fierceness in those black eyes in years.

I was still adjusting to the fleeting emotions that swirled in my body. Tears rose, but I didn't want to cry. I wanted to scream. "You don't think I considered it?" My voice cracked. "I know it's the easy way out."

"It's the *only* way!"

"No, it's not!" I screamed back. "There's always

another way. You know that just as much as I do." My mind raced for any shred to argue more. "How can you even be sure they'd agree? The sirens aren't going to just hand over my soul for nothing in return."

"I don't plan to go to them empty-handed," he replied tersely.

I shook my head. My chest heaved with hot, angry breaths as I read his face. "What could you possibly–" Still blocking the door, I reached for my sheath that hung next to it and my dagger slipped from its home with a quick *schwing*. I pointed the tip right at him. "Over my dead body."

"Dianna..."

My tears actually felt cold against the heat building in my cheeks. "Need I remind you what got us in this situation in the first place? The *reason* why I don't have my soul?" He hung his head. "Because I traded it for *you*, Henry. To save you! And now you're just going to hand yourself back to them?"

"No," he replied and took in a long inhale as he eyed me. "Just my soul."

In a bramble of anger, I flung the dagger at his feet and let the tears give way. "You bastard!"

"Christ, Dianna," he stepped toward me, but I swung my arms at his chest.

"No!" I screamed. "I won't let you! You can't, Henry, you can't! I just got you back!" He forced his arms around me, but I planted my feet firmly. "What about the kids?!"

"The kids need their mother!" He pulled away and grabbed hold of my flailing arms. "Let me do this for you!"

"You don't think I miss them?" I shrieked. "That I don't ache with every god damn fibre of my body to hold them in my arms?"

He tried to tug me toward him, but I slammed my back up against the door, only for it to push at me from behind. I stumbled forward. Finn barged in, followed by Benjamin, and they searched the room frantically.

"What the devil is goin' on in here?" Finn churred. "Ye woke every bloody person in the place!"

I wiped the wetness that ran from my eyes and nose and motioned my chin at Henry. "Ask him! He's the one about to trot off and hand his soul over to the sirens in exchange for mine!"

Henry's head tipped back, and he stared at the ceiling with an impatient sigh. "Jesus, Dianna, you don't need to involve them."

"Don't I?" I stared wide-eyed at him, madness pressing from under my skin.

"But..." Ben spoke, and we all whipped our heads. He had a weary, calculated expression on his face. "You'd be stuck here."

"I belong here, anyway," Henry replied calmly. "In this time."

"You belong with *me*!" I screamed, echoing words he once swore to me.

I turned to Finn and Ben for backup. But the two

of them stood like helpless game in the forest, unsure where to go or what to do. Each of them humming with the urge to leave. I wouldn't give them the satisfaction of being the first. I ripped my coat from the hook on the wall and stormed out.

CHAPTER SIXTEEN

I stomped around the little trader market that sat between the port and the village. Anger festered in my gut and I could practically taste it on my tongue. The sun was high in the sky and beamed down me, provoking a breakout of sweat in the most unsightly places. But I didn't care. I was aching inside. Betrayed by the one person I loved most in this world. After everything I'd done for him, he was just going to toss it all away. How could he do this to me?

No, he was doing it *for me*.

I knew that. But the anger I failed to rein in wouldn't let me accept it. I wove in and out of the dirty canvas tents and wobbly tables that displayed the latest goods to come in on pirate ships. I spotted that bone-carved comb I'd attempted to steal a few days prior, and I picked it up to admire in the sunlight.

"Beautiful comb for a beautiful lady?" the merchant said in a broken English accent.

I considered it for a moment before fetching a few coins from my pocket and reached over the table to place them in his palm. They must have been more than enough because he stared at the payment with wide, incredulous eyes before giving me a gracious nod.

"Good to see you're paying for things now," a gruff voice said in my ear.

I whirled around to find Benjamin alone—thank god—and I stuffed my purchase in the pocket of my jacket. "Are you always following me? Or only when I'm in a self-destructive mood?"

His reply was a shrug.

"Come to reason for him?"

He held up both hands in mock surrender. "Would never dream of it."

"I suppose he's already gone after the sirens," I replied and began walking away from the tent. I hated the way each word clipped with stubbornness.

"No," Ben said. "He and Finn headed off to discuss things that apparently I'm not part of."

"Freya?"

"She and the deckhands rowed back to the ship," he told me, and toed the dirt with his boot. "I guess they figure we'll be leaving soon."

I chortled and stared out at the ocean in the distance. Either I'd be aboard that ship, or Henry would. But not both of us. It was only a matter of who was more stubborn.

"How was Henry planning to send you back, anyway?" he asked. An odd and curious twitch in his brow.

"He...has a pearl." The word tasted like poison on my tongue. A pearl that was given to my *daughter*.

We paced along together and he seemed distant as he thought. "Can I take you somewhere?" Benjamin asked hesitantly. His hands were in his pockets as he rocked back on the heels of his boots.

"Where?"

He wore a smile that didn't reach his eyes. "Now, can't ruin the surprise, can I?"

It was impossible to be angry around the man. I knew I should head off to find my husband, to make amends and come to some sort of agreement. To reason with him. We'd find a way, I was sure of it. He just had to be patient while we searched. But this could very well be one of the last times I got to spend time with my friend before our lives changed yet again.

I huffed a sigh and smiled. "Lead the way, Mr. Cook."

I followed him away from the village, far from the bustling afternoon port, across the many beaches that lined the area. Until we crossed a grassy meadow and emerged on the other side of the tiny island, and a new, untouched beach sparkled in the sunlight. Not a sign of life to be found for miles.

"Jesus, Ben," I said, exasperated by the heat. "What kind of surprise is this? Putting me out of my misery so I don't have to deal with the tragedy that is my life?"

He stopped and turned with a look of pain. "That's not funny."

I straightened my back and immediately regretted the words. He'd already put me out of my misery once that week. "I'm sorry—"

His hand waved at the air between us. "Don't worry," he said and turned his gaze to the water. "Hopefully, this will set everything right."

His strong, calloused hand slipped around mine and I let him lead me to the water's edge. Confusion swept over me and I searched the sand, the water, then Ben's movements for any sign of what was to come. When he took a knife from his belt and drug it across his palm, I yelped.

"What the hell are you doing?" I shrieked and grabbed hold of his arm.

Calmly, he placed a hand over mine and released his arm with a smile. "Something I should have done a long time ago."

He knelt in the sand and put his bleeding palm in the water as he whispered words I couldn't hear or understand. "Seneca once told me this was the fastest way to summon a siren to you."

"Ben!" The sundried skin around my eyes burned with the sting of tears.

He stood over me, nothing but love in those soft brown eyes. A figure already moved in the water, heading right for us. It was all happening so fast. *Too fast*. My heart raced in its cage and my pulse pounded in my ears. Words evaded me. I couldn't stop it, because it was already happening. Quicker than I could process.

"Let me do this for you," Benjamin whispered soothingly. He seemed so at peace with his decision. But I was falling apart inside, and my grief was spilling out of me, pooling on the sand around me.

The siren reared her head; a muddled shape of water with two shadowed holes for eyes. She waded closer and closer, revealing more of her fluid body until it dried in the sun. Clear liquid making way to form a skin of pearl and hair of kelp so green and dark it almost looked black. Her gnarled, toothy grin widened.

"You offer me your blood, Benjamin Cook?" the sea beast's voice chimed in the air.

"I have," Ben replied confidently. Next to him, I trembled.

"The summon requires a trade." Her unnerving glassy eyes solidified to massive black pearls as she cocked her head to a fro like a wild animal assessing its prey.

"And a trade I have," he told her. "A soul."

"Ben..." The word died on my lips.

He looked at me, his face so utterly peaceful. I'd never witnessed him look that way before. "Don't pretend this isn't the right decision, Dianna."

My shoulders cinched up to my ears, and I shook

my head. "How can you ask me to be okay with this?"

"Because it's what I want," he replied. "For the first time in a lifetime, I finally know what I want to do. What I was...what my purpose is."

"Ben...I sailed across the sea and fought in the realm of monsters to get your soul–"

"So I could gift it back to you when the time was right," he said and took both my hands in his. The blood from his fresh wound trickled into my palm. "I see it now. Henry made me realize it this morning." I just stared at him in disbelief as the creature paced an impatient semi-circle around us. "I don't need to travel through time, I have no need for a mortal soul now that you've released me from my own curse. I'm free. And you did that. Don't you see, Dianna?"

My hands turned to ice and trembled in his firm grip. Tears spilled from my eyes, so much that I could hardly see his smile through the blur of them.

He pulled me closer. "You saved me from that ship and, in a way, from myself. You got my soul back and now it's time to repay that grand favor. I'll spend the rest of eternity knowing I did something right for all the awful things Abraham made me do aboard The Black Soul. You're my saviour, Dianna." He brought my hands to his face and kissed my knuckles, breathing warmth back into them.

Without a second thought, I leaned in and placed a long kiss at the corner of his mouth. Part of me expected him to react, to put his lips on mine and steal the kiss. But, like the eternal gentleman he was, Benjamin didn't move. I left the stain of my touch on his face and pulled away slowly, taking in his eyes as I did. His body remained cool, staid. But in that deep stare...I felt the fiery intensity displayed in the hollow shadows of wood and leather.

"I'll never forget this," I whispered.

"Thankfully, you'll only have the rest of your mortal life to think about it," he kidded, and I let a clumsy laugh push away the last of my tears. He turned to the silent beast that hovered next to us. "Do it."

Her fingers lengthened into thin claws. "You must say the words."

Benjamin stepped back from me and took a deep breath. "I, Benjamin Cook, trade my soul in exchange for the immediate return of Dianna Cobham's. No strings, no other conditions or underlying details." His eyes narrowed. "No curses. Just a clean trade."

Not needing any further prompting, the beast's fingers lengthened even more, the tips of them fading into pure moonlight as they dug into his chest. I covered my mouth to stifle the scream that lived in my throat because I knew exactly what it felt like. Like dying, followed by eternal bliss. Benjamin's back arched, his arms hung at his sides, and his mouth opened with a silent cry. And just as quick as it began, it was over. He bent over and braced his hands on his knees.

I reached for him, but the siren slammed her hands against my chest with a force unlike anything I'd ever felt before, and a blinding white light filled my vision. It knocked the wind from my lungs, and I flew back onto the sand with a mighty huff as I gasped for breath. When the light subsided, Benjamin's face hovered over me and his hair dangled across my cheeks.

"Are you alright?' he asked and helped me to my feet.

A strange weight that wasn't there before now sat snugly in my chest. My soul. It stretched as if alive, spread through to my limbs. I flexed my fingers in awe and my heart settled, knowing it didn't have to carry the load anymore.

I nodded. "Yeah, I'm..." I shook my head, still stunned at how fast, how simple the whole process was. "I'll be fine. Are you..."

Benjamin held his arms out with a giddy smile and then let them slap at his sides. "I'm alive." My mouth gaped helplessly for something to say. But what do you say to someone who quite literally saved your soul? He cocked his head in the direction we came from. "Go on. Use Henry's pearl and get home to your kids." His breath hitched in his chest. "Live happily ever after." I followed his gaze as it turned to the wide-open ocean before us. "I think...I think I'm going to give it a try."

I took Ben's warm hand and squeezed as the breeze whipped through our hair, across our faces.

I gave him one last smile, let it linger and last. Let him take in the sight of me one last time while I did the same to him. "You've got forever to figure it out."

His mouth widened with a smile. This time, reaching his eyes. "I've already got a good head start."

There was nothing more to say. Slowly, I let his hand fall from my grip, and the muscles of his arm tensed as I gave it a gentle squeeze before I walked past him. He remained on the beach, and I never once turned back to see if he was watching. I wanted to remember him not with a last look of longing, but with that content and genuine smile. I'd hold it in my heart for the rest of my time on this earth. In life, and even in death.

And maybe even after that.

THE END

IF YOU LOVED CANDACE OSMOND'S DARK TIDES SERIES BE SURE TO LEAVE A REVIEW WHEREVER BOOKS ARE SOLD!

AND FOLLOW CANDACE ON SOCIAL MEDIA FOR FUTURE UPDATES ON THE **DARK TIDES WORLD**.

"A Time Travel Series to Give Outlander a Run for its Money!"
⭐⭐⭐⭐⭐ - *InD Tale Magazine*

WANT EXCLUSIVE AUTHOR CANDACE OSMOND READER MERCH? SIGNED PAPERBACKS, HARDCOVERS, CHARACTER ART, AND MORE?

THEN CHECK OUT **DEATH BY READING**, CANDACE'S MERCH SHOPPE ON ETSY!

WANT MORE **TIME TRAVEL FANTASY ROMANCE**? CHECK OUT CANDACE'S NEXT SERIES, **KINGDOM OF SAND & STARS!**

Love is a weakness, even for the Gods.

Young archaeologist, Andie Godfrey must conquer her addiction and accept the opportunity to uncover the Egyptian cave where her father and boyfriend were last seen two years ago. But the pain of the past is hard to forget when you're thrown at its feet.

Using her father's secret research, Andie pieces together a clandestine conspiracy, centuries old, that will shatter the world's idea of ancient Egypt. But before she can solve her father's cryptic puzzle, Andie's betrayed by the leader of the expedition, and finds herself left for dead at the bottom of a pit where she accidentally activates a portal carved in stone.

Unsure whether she's dead or thrown back in the midst of time, Andie discovers an advanced civilization unlike anything she's ever known and is soon faced with a ruler among Gods; a man from her own past who once ruled her heart.

READ ON FOR A SNEAK PEEK!

Love was a complex creature. An ever-changing beast of emotions and promises. And we, like the gluttons for pain we are, crave love as it craves us, and then die with it when we let it burn out.

I knew this. I wasn't a fool.

But as I stood there on the terrace of my father's old Victorian townhouse and drank in the otherworldly beauty of the man before me, I happily accepted my fate. I'd let my love for him set me afire until there was nothing left but a pile of ash.

He was so worth the burn.

Silas gripped the edge of the wrought iron railing as he cast his face up to the moon and closed his eyes, drinking in the pale glow that poured down on us with a loving hunger. The moonlight enhanced everything about the man. The golden sheen hidden in his dark brown waves. The flawless skin that covered his body, like the color of wet sand drying in the sun. I watched intently, carving out every feature; his pointed nose, sharp jaw, the soft lips of his wide mouth. Finally, Silas opened his large eyes. Two dark holes lined with hints of mossy gold and looked to me standing in wait.

"You always do that," I said and shifted closer, our hands touching as our fingers wrapped around the railing together.

Silas regarded me innocently, mirroring the smile I gave him. "Do what?"

"Look at the moon like that. As if–" I shrugged with a grin. "As if you're in love with it."

Silas laughed. An infectious sound that always tickled my heart. "Perhaps I am."

"Are you saying I should be worried?" I slapped his arm and gave a mock look of surprise.

He turned then and gently grabbed me by the waist, pulling my body tight against his. The warmth and nearness of Silas melted my bones and I became putty in his arms. A place I'd happily stay forever. He looked intently into my eyes and I saw something I never witnessed there before. Something I couldn't quite put my finger on. An inkling that touched the bottom of my gut and registered the seriousness of the words that must have been rolling around in his mind.

"Never," he replied in a whisper that brushed across my face. "You don't ever have to worry about the way I feel for you, Andie." His long fingers slowly tucked a loose strand of hair behind my ear as he sighed thoughtfully. Distantly. "I love you."

I felt my cheeks fill with color as I ran my own fingers through his silky, haphazard waves. I tried to ignore the tinge of sadness I heard in those last three words and forced an uneasy smile.

"I love you, too. A part of me always has. Even when I was younger, I just...I just didn't understand the complexity of what I was feeling."

Three years ago, the university bestowed an assistant upon my father, the brilliant Alistair Godfrey. Scientist, archeologist, professor, well-known recluse, suddenly had a young field assistant who hardly left his side. Some say it was the best choice he ever made as his research advanced years overnight. His digs were always fruitful, and people came from all over the world to study under his teachings of Egyptian history and mythology at Dal.

That field assistant was Silas.

I remembered the very day he walked in the front door three years ago. I was a sullen and bitter fifteen-year-old, but something awakened inside me that day. Something warm and alive. I recognized him as one of Dad's students, but he seemed different somehow. Older, even though he was barely nineteen. They'd just returned from their first dig over near the coast of the Red Sea. Dad had grumbled before the trip, saying that the university was making him take Silas as part of some field study portion of the class. But they returned with some sort of unspoken understanding between them. Silas never left my father's side after that. And I secretly fell more in love with him with each passing day.

"I know." Silas sighed through the heavy silence that hung between us as he gently nodded, his eyes lost in some place I'd never get to see. "I ignored it at first, this...feeling. Your father would have killed me if he knew..."

More silence carried in the nighttime breeze that whipped around our faces. I inhaled a deep breath of that crisp cool air, let it fill my lungs. Despite the happy occasion, I couldn't shake the strange sense of dread that marked his every word. That flashed across his face when he looked in my eyes.

"Are we going to tell him before you guys leave?"

Silas's thick dark brow arched. "We leave first thing tomorrow."

"So? Let's tell him tonight," I said anxiously, desperate to prove to myself that nothing was wrong. "Let's go wake him up."

I pursed my lips at his quiet laughter and Silas took one of my hands. He stared down at it thoughtfully, mulling my fingers through his. "I'd rather we have something more to tell him. Something more than just the fact that we've been dating behind his back for the last year and a half."

My eyes rolled involuntarily. "Us dating is about as much news as my father can handle at one time, Silas."

The corner of his mouth twitched as he stifled a smile, one that surely never would have reached his eyes, even if he let it. "Still. I think we should wait. This trip will be the biggest discovery of your father's career. He cannot have distractions."

I blew out a huff of impatience as I rested my head against his warm chest. "Yeah, if you guys even find what you're looking for."

Silas waited a few beats before responding. "We will."

I pulled back and glanced up at his vacant face. Unsure if I should say anything. But I saw then, all the emotion he'd driven from his expression had pooled in his big green eyes and glistened in the moonlight. Happiness mixed with uncertainty.

"Silas, what's wrong?"

His brow creased in confusion. "What do you mean?"

"I'm not an idiot." I tipped my head to the side. "I can tell something's up. Tomorrow is the biggest day of Dad's career. Of both your careers. You guys have worked toward this for nearly three years. This tomb they found..." I shook my head to gather my thoughts. "What you guys find in there could change history as we know it."

I tried to inch away, to give myself breathing room, but Silas refused to let me go. His hands kept a firm grasp on the small of my back, pressing me against him. As if he were afraid to let me go. So, I let him hold me.

"What I'm getting at is that you should be excited," I continued and spread my hands out to smooth the hard lines of his back as we swayed to the gentle sounds of Etta James cooing from the tiny speaker on the old glass patio table.

"Do I not seem excited?"

My eyes widened. "Seriously? Silas, I don't know where you've been all night, but it hasn't been here."

I slipped one of my arms back from around his waist and cupped his cheek in my hand, willing him to come back to me. My thumb brushed the stressed skin under his eye and then slid down to his lips where I traced the perfect, sharp ridge that lined them. It always fascinated me. Slowly, I reached up on my toes and touched my mouth to his and sighed internally when those lips pressed hard against mine.

Breathless, I pulled back and gleamed up at him. "Just come back to me."

Finally, Silas's mouth widened with a smile that pulled his distant gaze back to the moment. "I never left. I've always been right here. With you. *For* you."

His arms, lean but more than able, scooped me up and spun around the spacious balcony before he set me down and left another slow, warm kiss on my lips. I watched as he then reached into the inside pocket of his leather jacket and pulled out a tiny black velvet satchel, pulled closed with a thin drawstring. Glancing down at it in his hand, the other still holding me tightly, he seemed to be contemplating his next words carefully.

"Tomorrow, your father and I leave on a trip that could take me away from you for a long time."

"Yeah, I know," I replied with a shrug. "I know it's dangerous. No one's ever been down there. You don't know what you're going to find. I get it. But I'll come visit during my breaks." I suddenly regretted registering for the summer program to shorten my course length. The sadness began to seep back into his eyes, and I urged him with mine. "It won't be so bad, I promise. And I'm sure Dad will give you breaks to fly home. It's only fair."

He guffawed. "Nothing is ever fair."

I chose to ignore that statement and let him

continue, leaning back as he pulled open the drawstrings on the small bag. I watched as he turned it over and dumped the contents into his palm. A beautiful pendant, a jagged and cloudy gemstone partially encased in gold where it attached to a thick chain. Silas looped it around his finger as he held it up to dangle in front of me. It was gorgeous. I stared in awe as the silver moonlight filtered through the milky stone, reflecting off the flawed particles and revealing what looked like a tiny universe inside it.

"What's this?" I asked in a breathy whisper. "It's amazing."

The corner of Silas's mouth quirked. "It's somewhat of a family heirloom. My mother gave it to me many years ago. This stone is very much a part of me, Andie. In more ways than I can properly explain." He moved to grab my hand and turn my palm up, open, to let the pendant pool heavy in the center. "I want you to have it. To take care of it while I'm away. *Never* let it go."

I stared down at the stunning piece of jewelry in my grip and my heart fluttered with all the possibilities of us. Of our future. Of my love for this man. Proudly, I looped the thick, yet lightweight chain over my head and felt the cold stone press against my chest. Directly over my rapidly beating heart.

"Thank you," I told Silas as I beamed up at him. "I'll never take it off."

He gently pressed on the pendant and I knew he

must have felt the hard thump of my wild heart beating through it. My breathing quickened, matching his, and we stood connected as our bodies fell in sync with every breath and beat.

I felt his chest vibrate with the deep hum of his voice as Silas leaned even closer, his hand firm against the back of my head and pulling me in. Our faces met with a new intensity, a deep burning heat that constantly smoldered under the surface, waiting to ignite. I threw my head back in sheer bliss as Silas's soft lips touched against the tender skin of my neck and sent a wave of goosebumps flourishing across the surface of my body, pooling in the center.

Absently, my hands worked to remove his leather jacket and lift the black long-sleeved shirt over his head, revealing the gorgeous shape of his lean muscles. Our lips hungrily danced together as he took a few steps forward, pushing me back against the heavy, glass patio table. I opened my legs, welcoming him, and Silas leaned into me as they wrapped around him tightly.

A devilish grin smeared across his face. "Andie," his voice smooth, those lips just a sliver away from mine. I mumbled some response, dizzy from the nearness of him. Silas nuzzled his face in my hair and his warm mouth lightly caressed my ear with a breathy whisper, "Happy birthday."

DIVE INTO THE KINGDOM OF SAND & STARS SERIES WITH ANCIENT HEARTS TODAY!

ABOUT THE AUTHOR

#1 International and *USA TODAY* Bestselling Author, Candace Osmond was born in North York, ON.
She published her first book by the age of 25, the first installment in a Paranormal Romance Trilogy called The Iron World Series.
Candace is also one of the creative writers for sssh.com, an acclaimed Erotic Romance website for women which has been featured on NBC Nightline and a number of other large platforms like Cosmo. Her most recent project is a screen play that received a nomination for an AVN Award.
Now residing in a small town in Newfoundland with her husband and two kids, Candace writes full time developing articles for just about every niche, more novels, and a hoard of short stories.

Connect with Candace online! She LOVES to hear from readers! *www.AuthorCandaceOsmond.com*

  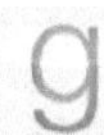